The GATE Was OPEN

To: Mark and Laurie

KEN ENGLAND

Copyright © 2023 Ken England
All rights reserved
First Edition

PAGE PUBLISHING
Conneaut Lake, PA

First originally published by Page Publishing 2023

ISBN 979-8-88654-148-9 (pbk)
ISBN 979-8-88654-150-2 (digital)

Printed in the United States of America

ACKNOWLEDGMENTS

This novel has to acknowledge my father—he struggled with this cruel and unforgiving disease. However, the most important part of this story is my mother, who cared for someone whose mind slowly faded from normal functioning to something totally unrecognizable. Also another very important part of the novel is everyone at Book Master's, with special thanks going to Shelly Sepyta.

CHAPTER 1

2005

Snow has very distinctive sounds when a person walks on it. A snow fall when the temperature is twenty below or colder has a very grating sound as the ice crystals grind together. The powder in a warmer snow often sloughs with a sound similar to someone pouring white refined sugar into a cup. But this morning, the snow was wet because the street surface was warm from the previous days of warmer weather. Therefore, a footfall made a squishy sound like stepping into a puddle. And the warmth of the road surface was one thing that saved the man from losing his feet to frostbite.

A late season snow had deposited a foot of snow on the town of Carolina Beach. The man weaved in and out of cars as he negotiated his way down the street. Another man was walking his dog up the sidewalk on the other side of the motorway. He glanced over at the man trying not to make it obvious that he was staring. Since the elderly man was weaving in and out of cars, the dog walker wondered if he was casing vehicles in an attempt to steal from them. Or more commonly, to steal the whole car. As the dog walker turned a corner and went behind a building, he quickly turned back and gave his dog a command while putting his finger to his month.

"Sit," he said as quietly as he could.

When the dog saw the sit signal, she immediately sat down and waited for her reward. The man fished in his pocket as the dog watched with increased interest. He also leaned around the corner of the building. The elderly man had continued his weaving, and to the watcher's amazement, when the man came out from between two parked cars, he was completely naked.

As the man continued to watch, he saw the elderly man's bare feet as he splashed through the wet snow.

This guy has got to be drunk, he thought.

He pulled out his iPhone and dialed 911.

"What's the location of your emergency?" the 911 operator said.

"Well, let's see… I just turned off Main Street unto…this is Bush Street."

"So you are at Main and Bush?"

"Yes, ma'am."

"What is your emergency?"

"Well, it's not my emergency but there is a drunk guy wandering around and he is butt naked. He is even barefoot."

"Is he injured?"

"Well, I don't know. I haven't talked to him, I am just calling this in because if he falls or something, he will never survive. I thought he was casing cars, but when I noticed he was completely naked, I figured it was something else."

"Okay, sir. I will dispatch law enforcement."

"Thank you."

The man walking his dog decided to stay and watch the scenario unfold. Within five minutes, a police cruiser came down the street with the light bar flashing. Then the spotlight came on, and the man leaning up against the side of the building was temporarily blinded. He shielded his eyes with his hand and pointed across the street. The spotlight swung over to the parked cars. The naked man emerged between two cars and immediately turned around and walked with his back to the light. The officer jumped out of his squad car with a large flashlight.

"Police, hands up where I can see them," the officer shouted with his flashlight on the naked man. The man kept walking oblivious to anything around him.

"Sir, sir put your hands behind your head and freeze."

THE GATE WAS OPEN

The man with the dog was watching and chuckled at the command to *freeze*. It was about thirty degrees out, and the man was walking completely naked in slushy snow.

The police officer approached cautiously with his hand gun drawn and at the ready. He eased up to the elderly man and with one hand grabbed the old man's arm and then holstered his weapon. He pulled out one set of his handcuffs then cuffed one of the man's wrists to his other wrist. As he was cuffing, the subject he noticed what looked like a very fancy watch. The light was low, and Daren brought the watch up to a place that he could see it.

R-O-L-E-X. Rolex. Wow, I've never seen one of these before. I wonder who this guy is? he thought.

Then the police officer walked him around to the squad car and put him in the back seat. He walked around to the trunk and got a blanket out, opened the back door and handed the elderly man the blanket.

An officer Daren Kent had seen a lot of strange things on his five years on the force, but an elderly man walking around totally naked was a new one on him.

I would rather have seen something else. he thought. Oh well, at the age of twenty-five, he was still single, but it wasn't for lack of trying. He opened the driver's side door and climbed in the car.

"Sir, wrap yourself up in that blanket."

"Where's Mom?"

"What?" Daren asked.

"Where's Mom?"

Daren chuckled because he thought this old man could be looking a long time for his mom.

"Whose mother are you talking about?"

There was no response.

"Hey, it's cold out here, bundle yourself up in that blanket. I guess that's kinda hard to do when your cuffed."

Officer Kent took the corners of the blanket and tucked them behind the man's back, and he could feel the itchy wool on his skin, but there wasn't anything he could do about it.

The man sat in silence.

Wow, this guy must be drunker than fifty alcoholics, he thought. That's when Daren decided to do a breathalyzer on the guy. He pulled the device out of its case and inserted a new mouthpiece into the intake port.

"Blow into this tube, sir."

"Where's Mom?" the man asked.

"For the last time, I don't know where your mom is."

Daren held the breathalyzer up to the man's mouth. "Now, blow into this tube."

The man's head turned sideways with that command. He had a confused look on his face. Daren rolled his eyes and sighed an audible sigh.

"Look, we can do this the easy way or the hard way. You are going to end up in jail if you don't comply with this test."

"I want Mom."

"Shit, this guy is like a broken record. Okay, I am going to take you to the hospital to make sure you are okay."

"Sorry."

"Wow, now you are sorry."

"Sorry."

"It's 593, 63."

"Go ahead, 63."

"Can you dispatch the ambulance to this location?"

"The ambulance is tied up on a medical emergency, 63."

"How about the backup EMS crew?"

"Out of service, 63."

"Okay, I am going to transport this person to the ER."

"Ten-Four, 63. What is the patient's medical condition?"

"Unknown, could be drunk, could be some other problem like a mental instability."

"Did you do a breathalyzer on this patient?"

"Negative, 593. Subject refusing."

"Ten-four, 63."

Daren reached into the back seat and buckled the man's seat belt. Daren pulled into the half circle in front of the ER entrance.

Then he walked in and got a wheelchair and brought that out to his car. He opened the door and looked in at the elderly man.

"What is your name, sir?"

The man merely stared back at him. Officer Kent glanced at the watch on the man's wrist and as he stood outside of his car, he glanced to the east and he could tell the sky was lightening and he knew the sun would break the horizon in about an hour. He wheeled the chair up to the front desk.

"This man needs to be seen immediately."

"What's going on with him?" the registration person asked.

"He seems to be delusional, and he was walking around in his birthday suit and barefooted."

"Does he have any ID?"

At that point the blanket swung off the man's shoulder and fell to the ground. After working in the ER for a number of years, nothing surprises you. The man was sitting on the wheelchair completely naked.

"If you can find his ID, let me know because I need that info too."

"Well, for now we will have to call him John Doe," she responded. "You want to wrap him up and take him back to room three."

The officer led him back into the emergency room and took him into room three where they were met by an RN.

"What do we have here?" she inquired.

"I picked this man up down town walking around totally naked and barefoot in the cold and snow."

"Has he been shivering?" the nurse asked.

"Not that I have noticed," the officer said.

"Well, I will get a temp on him," she said after she got him on the stretcher. "Can you put that Bear Hugger on him?"

"The what?" Officer Kent said.

"That puffy air mattress over there," she said.

The thermometer beeped and she removed it from his ear canal.

"Wow! Ninety-seven point one degrees. That's incredible, maybe he just walked outside a minute ago."

"Well, I've been dealing with him for at least ten minutes, but I think your biggest problem is he is obviously out of it. Could that be possible with a temperature of ninety-seven?"

"Not likely."

"Well, I am going to keep my money on alcohol."

"Yeah, but it could be a lot of other things too."

She pressed on his feet and each one of his toes and felt the pliability of normal tissue. "His feet don't look or feel frostbitten."

The nurse had been working in the ER for ten years and had never seen anyone as ambivalent to the sensations that one would expect. He was completely unfazed by the cold.

"He refused the breathalyzer, so we don't have an alcohol level on him yet."

"Well, I will draw a BA on him, and we can at least clear that up."

"You are going to have to help me out with the medical acronyms."

"That's a blood alcohol level, and that is what we will need to answer your question. Could you change his cuffs around to the front? And you can hold his arm still while I get this blood sample."

"Sure, I'll help you out."

"And you don't have any identification you this guy."

"No, he was naked as a jaybird and the only thing he has on him is that watch, but I think it's one of those very pricey ones."

"Has he said anything that would identify him?"

"The only thing he has said is 'Where's Mom?' and 'Sorry,' and I have heard those two things more times than anyone should have to."

"So a lot of repetitive speech, and who is 'Mom'?" Katie inquired.

"That's a good question, and if you can figure that one out, you will be my hero. Why don't you ask him?"

The man perked up and looked around the hospital room.

"Mom! Where's Mom?"

"Sir, my name is Katie, and I am taking care of you. Can you tell me who Mom is?"

"Where's Mom?"

"Sir, we don't know if you are referring to your mom or somebody else's mom. Do you know Mom's name?"

The man just sat there and stared straight ahead. As he sat there, his fingers began to tap out a rhythm as if he was playing something. This activity went unnoticed by everyone around him. Katie drew his blood while Daren held his arm straight.

When the needle punctured the vein in the bend of his elbow, he said, "Ouch! You damaged my arm!"

"No, sir. Your arm will be just fine. Wow, that's the most we have heard out of him!"

"You got that right. I think he is responding better to a woman. Why don't you try finding out some more info?"

"Sir, do you know what day it is?" She waited and got no response.

"Do you know where you are?" She waited again, still nothing.

"Sir, what time is it?"

The man looked at his watch and counted the numbers on the face of the watch.

"Six-thirty," he said.

"Whoa." She looked at the clock on the wall. "That's right, very good. So what's your name?"

"Roscoe."

"All right. Hello, Roscoe. I am Katie. We are two for two. What is your last name?"

The mam just sat there and starred at her again.

"What day is it, Roscoe?"

He looked at the watch again and traced the numbers with his finger again. They held their breath in the ER.

"Six-thirty," he said.

"Oh well, thought we were on a roll. I guess that's alert and oriented times two or maybe one and half."

CHAPTER 2

1960

The heat was heavy and the humidity was thick. The sweat trickled down his face, and the salt stung his eyes as he walked down the busy street to the music store. Roscoe always wanted to play the organ, but his aunt had an old piano down in her basement, and she lived right down the street from him and his mom. His mom was constantly having to pinch pennies especially since his dad left. His mom took the less expensive option and had him play his songs on the free piano in his aunt's house. Roscoe's mom, Cindy, would walk down to her sister's house with him every day after school, and while he was downstairs playing his chords, Mom and Auntie Ellen were upstairs drinking as much wine as they could get down. Or more than likely, they would run out of wine. Roscoe eventually figured out that he could play entire songs with just four chords.

    The owners of the music store were Nate Kovolesky and his sister who was never there. Nate had played the piano for many years. He taught Roscoe all the old ragtime classics. Nate was a very rotund man who looked a lot like a beluga. But when he got to playing his piano, he seemed to come alive and the music freed him. His whole body would get into the music and everything would be jiggling. Roscoe would call him Mr. Nate after he was told that Mr. Kovolesky just wouldn't do. Roscoe loved going to the music store because he could escape the anxiety and problems at home when he played his lessons for Nate.

THE GATE WAS OPEN

When he went down to his aunt's house to practice, he would have to support his mom on the way home. But Roscoe was oblivious to the trauma especially when he was in front of the keyboard. He slowly mastered the subtle flow of tickling the ivories. Roscoe played whenever he could and had a lesson with Nate every week. Nate immediately realized the boy was a protégé. Each week, he gave his excited student something more, and Roscoe snapped it up like a hungry dog. Some pieces he would look at and play flawlessly the first time. And then for the rest of the week, he would clean it up until he reached perfection. Luckily for Roscoe, he was born with a super memory, which got him through school on a wing and a prayer. Except one class and that was music class. The teacher in music was Beth Ellef, and she was incredibly impressed with this young virtuoso. Between his school music teacher and Nate, they had a young musical genius on their hands. Every song was another great challenge for him, and his teachers scrambled around to find new challenges.

At some point though, his mother's drinking was destroying the family—she had wrecked three cars and lost two jobs. The family was destitute, and the first thing to go was Roscoe's piano lessons.

Cindy approached Nate and said, "Mr. Kovolesky, Roscoe can't take lessons from you anymore."

Ten-year-old Roscoe Gillette began to tear up, and he thought he had done something wrong.

"But, Mrs. Gillette, he is, hands down, my best student. When he gets older, he will be making a lot of money but only if he keeps practicing," he said. As he spoke he could smell the alcohol emitting from her breath and from every pore on her skin.

"Well, we just don't have the money to keep paying you," she said, slurring her words.

"You know Roscoe is good enough that he could start playing gigs."

"Really?" she said, her eyes lighting up.

Nate immediately knew he had said the wrong thing. If this child started making money playing, his mother would collect it all for herself and probably drink herself into an early grave. Cindy had been a singer in the past, and she knew about the potential earning power of a good band.

"Come on, Mom. I want to do those things. I can do it."

"I know you can, sweetie." Then she looked at Nate. "Can you set up these events?"

"Well, I have a wedding next month, but I play the piano, so there is no need for another piano player."

"I have a niece getting married soon. Roscoe can play at the one," she said.

"Do you have a piano?"

"My sister does, but it is in her basement."

"Well, there might be one at the reception, you should check into that."

"Yeah, you are right. The reception is in the basement of the church, and there is a piano down there."

Nate was depressed, knowing that he had gotten Roscoe into a life of child slavery to feed his mother's addiction.

Within a couple months, Roscoe was playing at his cousin's wedding. It was quite a good time especially for Cindy Gillette, and she got very drunk and passed out at the wedding. Nate had showed up incognito to see if Roscoe was progressing in his music. Roscoe was ripping off everything from ragtime to jitterbug classics. But right then Nate realized he would do much better with some other musicians in his band to fill in. Definitely a lead guitarist, bass, and drums. Nate started making calls to friends in the music world around the area.

Soon the band came together and met in Nate's garage. The large door on the garage was off the tracks and didn't work. The only way into the garage was through the backdoor, and the group batted around many names and Roscoe came up with the Backdoor Brothers. Eventually, that stuck and the group began to be known as that. They practiced every week in Nate's garage. Nate had an old piano in the garage, and once he and Roscoe did some repair work on it, they had it ringing out some classic tunes.

By the time Roscoe was ten, he was a professional musician, and the group didn't have to do anymore fast talking to play in bars. By that time, Backdoor Brothers had cut their first album, which was called *Pacifier*. Nate became the manager of the band, and he worked with Roscoe on the side to refine his skills.

However, the young man was already very skilled, and Nate spent his time teaching Roscoe new songs. The one thing they were lacking was a singer, and that's when Roscoe said, "My mom can sing."

Cindy started touring with the band because she was there anyway to take care of Roscoe, which was getting less and less necessary. But Cindy Gillette was totally unreliable. One night while performing, she fell off the stage, and the bar owner threw them out and then asked them not to come back. That bar was one of their best gigs, and at that point, Nate was forced to make a decision, which took place the next day.

"Cindy, I need to talk to you."

"What's up, big man?"

"You got drunk and fell off the stage last night."

"No, I didn't. I just slipped."

"You were shit-faced drunk and slurring your words. And the entire band was embarrassed by you, especially Roscoe, he was crying."

"Bullshit. That boy loves his mother!"

"When you are drunk, you have no idea what you are doing and that child has carried you through your life."

"You don't know what you are talking about," she said.

"Well, you are done with this band. In other words, you are fired!"

"You can't do that."

"Well, I am afraid I can, I am the manager of this group. And I asked the rest of the band and they were all in favor of getting rid of you. You are making a joke out of us."

"All in favor, what about Roscoe?"

"He is only ten, so he doesn't get a vote," Nate said.

"Well, guess what, I am his mom, so if I leave your star piano player goes with me."

"I knew you would say that, and I am prepared to take over for Roscoe."

"And who's going to sing?"

"Someone who is a lot better than you."

She held up both of her middle fingers.

"That's what I think of you," she said.

"Cindy, here's your cut from last night's gig. Go to the hospital and get your injuries taken care of."

She grabbed the cash from his hand. "You are the biggest asshole I've ever known."

"Well, I've gotten you some info on a group known as Alcoholics Anonymous."

He handed her several pamphlets and a book written by a guy maned Bill W. She promptly threw the literature back in his face.

"Well, now you are definitely fired," Nate said.

"Me and my boy will start another band."

"Well, you will need a lot of money to pull that one off, and you and I know you will drink that all away."

All Nate could hope for was an early death for Cindy and maybe Roscoe would rejoin the Backdoor Brothers. Then they could all seek fame and fortune. But he didn't want to influence this event because his weight issues were taking a toll on him and slowing him down. He could probably manage the band for five more years.

CHAPTER 3

1960

Live music was everything to her, she listened to the popular music that all the kids were listening to. Then she branched out to listen to the new rock-and-roll. Rebecca Ribault was becoming a groupie. When she turned fifteen, she heard a new rock-and-roll band called the Backdoor Brothers, and she was hooked. Not only did she really like the music, but also there was a young boy who played the piano that was a total doll.

Becky looked a lot older then she really was. Which was convenient because the best live music was in bars and she had the look of an eighteen-year-old. Lucky for her, she had an older sister, and one day, she helped herself to her sister's driver's license.

"Have you seen my driver's license, Becky?" her sister asked.

"You know I don't drive!"

"Yeah but my purse was all messed up the other day, and you were the only one here."

"What are you accusing me of?" Becky responded.

"Look, all I'm saying is you were the only one here and then I went to a bar and they wanted to see my ID and I couldn't find it."

"Why do you always blame me for everything?" Becky asked.

"Because you always follow me around trying to horn in on my friends."

"I do not."

"I left, and when I got back, my purse was all messed up."

"I didn't do anything to your purse!"

The argument turned into a stalemate. Becky walked away with a grin on her face and her sister's ID in her pocket. She knew that her lazy sister just had to go back to the Department of Motor Vehicles to get a new copy of her driver's license. Becky started doing her hair like her sister so she looked like the photo on the ID. Then she had free access to any bar in town.

Becky was fifteen, and when she saw the youngest boy in the band, she fell head over heels in love with him. Little did she know that Roscoe was just a year older than her. While all the other young girls were screaming, Becky just melted into the crowd. She knew full well that she would have little chance with a big star, especially with so much competition screaming at him. Roscoe Gillette was a dream with blond hair and that very boyish charm that made all the girls swoon.

Becky made her way to the stage with a lot of squirming as well as pushing and shoving. She had gotten very good at weaseling her way through tight crowds. Then she found herself at the edge of the stage, with the throbbing crowd. And it just so happened that right above her was Roscoe Gillette playing the piano. When he looked at the crowd, the screams increased tenfold.

Becky had forgotten one key element of partying and that was to stay hydrated. She suddenly collapsed, and Roscoe immediately stopped playing and the rest of the band started looking around wondering what had happened to the piano. Roscoe stood on the edge of the stage pointing down into the crowd.

"Security," he yelled.

Nate looked up with the disturbance and was moving toward the stage. He struggled to get his three-hundred-pound bulk up the four stairs to the stage. The crowd was howling with the cessation of the music.

Nate walked over to the mike and spoke to the crowd, "Calm down, folks. We will get this figured out and get the music going again."

He walked over to where Roscoe was standing. "What's going on, buddy?"

"There's a girl down there who just passed out, and she's going to get trampled!" Roscoe responded.

"This kind of thing happens all the time at concerts. I'm sure that she is just drunk."

Roscoe had been dealing with his mother's alcoholism, and he had developed a soft heart for people afflicted by the demons that swirled in a bottle of alcohol.

"I got to help her," he said as he jumped down off the stage. The crowd drew its collective breath.

"Roscoe," Nate yelled Roscoe as he watched the star that he had been nurturing disappear into the crowd. Roscoe squatted down and lifted the girl's head. As he did that, her eyes opened, and she had a vision of a blond-haired god. The one thing that she had been dreaming of every night. He was holding her head like he was about to kiss her. That's when Becky took matters into her own hands. She raised her head and planted a kiss on Roscoe's lips. Roscoe, who was very inexperienced at the kissing game, felt his lips suddenly start tingling.

Wow, he thought. *What was that?*

By then, two burly security guards showed up, and one of them lifted Roscoe up to the stage. The other one was holding the crowd back. Roscoe was still stunned by that tingle on his lips. The ambulance crew was escorted in by more security, and they took Becky away to a hospital.

After the concert, Roscoe spoke to Nate. "I have to go check on that girl. Do you know where they took her?"

"To the hospital, I guess," Nate responded.

"What hospital?"

"Roscoe, neither of us are from around this area, so I don't where the hospital is."

"Well, I'll get a cab," Roscoe countered.

"Okay, well, if you want to check on this girl then I'll go with you."

"Well, let's go!"

Nate walked around making sure the roadies were starting to pack the equipment up. Roscoe grew impatient and wandered out of the arena to the street. He saw a cab approaching and raised his hand to signal his intent to hire the cab. The cab cruised right by him. He let a few expletives out. Then he saw another cab coming, and he waved his arm and the cab stopped in front of him.

"What is the closet hospital to here?" Roscoe inquired.

"Um, Memorial General is about five miles from here."

"Okay, let's go!"

The cabbie looked at the young man. "You got money, kid?"

Roscoe felt his face flush because when they were playing they never carried any money.

"Ah, no," he said.

"Well get out of my cab, you young punk."

Roscoe stepped back out to the sidewalk. He felt dejected, but he had to figure out a way to solve this problem without Nate's help. That's when he saw a group of people approaching. He collapsed onto the sidewalk and a couple of the guys walked over to him.

"You okay, man?" one of the guy's said to him.

"Help," Roscoe muttered out.

"What's wrong with you?"

"Hospital."

"There's a phone booth right there, I'll call an ambulance."

Ten minutes later, a hearse-style ambulance with a single revolving light on the top of it pulled up to the curb. The siren blared in his ears and was actually painful until the driver shut it off.

"What's wrong with you?" the EMT asked.

"All over."

The ambulance personnel looked at each other and shrugged.

"Do you want to go to the hospital?"

"Yes!"

They loaded him up on the gurney and wheeled him into the ambulance. Then they drove him to the hospital emergency and wheeled him through the swinging doors and into the brightly lit hospital.

Roscoe watched carefully as he was wheeled past other rooms, and then he suddenly saw the girl that had fallen at the concert. They kept going to a different room. A nurse came into the room and started asking him questions. Roscoe thought he was in a lot of trouble having lied to the ambulance technicians, and he was desperate to pull the plug on this deception.

"I'm feeling much better now," he said to the nurse.

"What do you mean you are feeling better, you called an ambulance."

"No, I didn't call the ambulance. Those other guys did," Roscoe said, trying to get out of this problem.

"Why did they call the ambulance?"

"I don't know," he said.

"And you let them put you in the ambulance for no reason?"

"I had some pain, but it is gone now. So I want to check out now."

"Well, where was your pain?"

Roscoe pointed to his abdomen, hoping that he could talk his way out of this farce.

"There are a lot of things that could be causing your pain that you should have checked out," the nurse said.

"I'll come back if it happens again."

"Where are your parents?"

"At the Backdoor Brothers concert," Roscoe answered.

"Okay, well, you can leave if you want to."

"Thank you, ma'am."

Roscoe got up quickly and got dressed, and he walked down the hallway. He wasn't sure which room the girl was in, and he pulled the curtain open to see an older woman with white hair. He quickly reversed his course and closed the curtain and walked down the hallway to the next room. Becky was lying on her side facing away from the curtain.

Roscoe walked up to the young woman and said, "Are you feeling better?"

She rolled over and her eyes got as big as dinner saucers. She was looking at the face of her favorite musician.

"Roscoe Gillette? Am…am I dreaming?"

"Well, if you dream with your eyes open, then maybe, but I just came by to see if you were doing all right."

"I can't believe this is happening," she said.

"When I saw you drop I was concerned you might have hurt yourself."

Becky was suddenly self-conscious, and she quickly straightened her hair and wiped away the tears that were inexplicably running down her cheeks. Roscoe kept looking around hoping not to be discovered by the nurse that he had just duped. Becky couldn't believe her hero was in her room.

"I, I don't know what to say," she got out between a few stutters.

"Well, I'm just reaching out to you because you were hurt while at my concert."

"I wasn't hurt. I just fainted, and thank you for helping me."

A different nurse came into Becky's room. She was surprised to see a visitor.

"Hi, who are you?" the nurse inquired.

"He is my boyfriend," Becky quickly said.

"Ah, yeah," Roscoe said, looking from Becky to the nurse.

"Well, Miss Ribault, if you are feeling better, you are free to leave."

"Yes, I feel better now, just a little embarrassed."

"Don't worry, sweetie. It could have happened to anyone," Roscoe said.

She immediately blushed mostly because of the term of endearment that he used. The nurse grinned at the young lovers.

"Well, sir, why don't you step out while she gets dressed."

"Okay," Roscoe said as he slipped out of the room.

"Wait for me," Becky pleaded.

"I'll be right out here," he said.

Becky was dressing so fast she put her bra on backward, and then, out of frustration, tore it off and threw it in the trashcan. Then slipped a tee shirt on. Then she walked out of her room and took his hand as they walked out of the emergency room. Roscoe's nurse looked up and seeing him, she said. "Oh, did you decide to get checked out?"

"No, it was great talking to you, but my girlfriend and I are in a hurry," he said. Then they exited the hospital.

"Girlfriend? He came in by ambulance. Where was she before?" the nurse muttered to herself.

"How do you know her?" Becky asked.

"Oh, just a fan, you know!"

"Well, she said something about an ambulance."

"Yeah, I got injured too, and I came here by ambulance. You know, an abundance of caution."

"What? Are you okay, baby?"

"Yeah, it turned out to be nothing," he chuckled.

"Do you have a car?"

"No, we travel by a bus. So what are we going to do now?"

She was trembling and grabbed his hand even tighter so he couldn't feel that?

"Well, we could do something fun," she said.

"Do you have any money?"

"A little," she said, a bit confused how a big star could be broke.

"I don't carry any money while I am performing."

She was so enamored by him. In other words, there was nothing she wouldn't do for him.

"Well, there is a motel right over there," she said biting her lip. "But aren't you on tour?"

Neither of them could believe that this had progressed to this stage.

"I'll catch up to them in the morning."

They checked into the motel.

CHAPTER 4

1960

The slamming door woke Becky up with a start.

"Roscoe," she muttered, then she realized she was alone, and she sat silent to listen for any sound like the shower running, but nothing.

Roscoe was jogging down the stairs of the motel, and even though he wasn't working that hard, he was sweating.

Man, she was really into that last night. She was screaming at the top of her lungs.

Neither of them knew what they were doing, and they tried to figure out all of the details. It was basically Part A into Part B. Because of the guttural screaming, he thought he was a lover of great repute. The thought of birth control never even crossed their minds. He was on top of the world having just lost his virginity.

Becky had just lost her virginity, too, to the man of her dreams. She could feel a change in her and knew that her life had just changed forever. She rolled over in the bed and threw the covers back and jumped out of the bed and ran to the window. She pulled the blinds to the side and stared out into the parking lot. Her mouth hung open as she tried to speak and then she knew she had done an amazingly bad thing. And she was afraid she might have lost the love of her life. Becky ran out of the room in her birthday suit, and when she didn't see Roscoe, a very shocking feeling came over her. She began hyperventilating and then she realized that there was a family standing right there, twenty five feet from her. She turned around and tried to get back into the room but the door had locked.

Becky felt the flushing starting, but unbeknownst to her, she was breathing very rapidly. The embarrassment was so complete she began to gag and the dry heaves started rocking her breasts. With one arm over her breasts and one hand over her crotch, she didn't know where to go, and the parents of the family were herding their children away, but the two kids kept turning around to look. The air was cool and she pulled the door knob to no avail.

Damn, my first time, and here I am, running around naked. This isn't supposed to happen. I thought Roscoe was going to be my one and only, she thought.

She ran down the stairs of the hotel and out through the parking lot to the street. She didn't want to go back into the motel office, totally naked. It was still early in the morning so the traffic was light but all the cars slowed and some stopped. Then a police car came up behind her and the loud speaker came to life.

"Ma'am, stay right there!" the officer said.

I thought I was going to make it, she thought as she leaned completely naked up against the police car.

"What are you doing out here?"

"Sorry, officer, I got locked out of my hotel room and I was trying to get to my car," she said doing the best she could to cover herself.

"Are you okay? Nothing bad happened to you?"

"Well, my boyfriend left me, so that was one bad thing."

"But you weren't assaulted or anything, were you?"

"No," she said feeling dejected, and felt she was being a victim and she was being given the third degree.

"Why didn't you go back to the office to get another key?"

"Because there is a weird guy in there. Hey, listen, do you have a bed sheet or something I could use to cover up with?"

"No sheet, but I do have a wool blanket."

"Okay, thanks," she replied.

He handed Becky the blanket and she wrapped herself up in it.

Becky was dealing with a hidden disorder; once she realized she was locked out of her room without a stitch of clothing, her stress skyrocketed. She was breathing at a rate of forty breathe per minute. Over the years, Becky was able to develop a very subtle, quiet, rapid respiration. The breathing was so quiet that no one noticed when it was happening. Her hands started tingling immediately then she became dizzy and then standing by the patrol car with the officer, she fainted.

The officer had turned around to help her keep her dignity while she wrapped herself in the blanket. He had not noticed her breathing. Then her head started spinning and the next thing the cop knew, she collapsed to the pavement. He quickly called for an ambulance. It was 1965 and the ambulance responded was a Cadillac station wagon. These were also used as a hearse, but when they were used as ambulances they had a single red revolving light on top. The two technicians loaded her on a stretcher. Then the two guys hopped into the front of the ambulance and drove at high speed to the hospital. Becky was strapped to the stretcher but was still thrown around when the vehicle went around corners.

When Becky was taken out of the ambulance and rolled into the emergency room. The doctor was familiar with this condition especially in young girls.

"You have to breathe into this bag," he said. He took a paper bag and opened it and held it over Becky's mouth. She panicked and pushed the bag away.

"Ma'am, you have to let me help you. You will feel much better if you just listen to what I say. You will be able to breathe just fine."

He put the bag over her mouth again and as she calmed down and breathed, the bag inflated then deflated. Once she realized that this was not going to kill her, she let it happen. Eventually, the dizziness dissipated and her hands stopped tingling.

"Now, how did you end up walking around the town naked?"

"Got locked out of my hotel room."

"And how did you get locked out of your hotel room?"

She just turned her head to the side tired of this game that everyone was obviously into playing.

"Well, you just rest, and the next time you step out of your motel room make sure you grab some clothes."

* * *

Roscoe got back to the tour bus and Nate was freaking out.

"Where the hell have you been? I was looking all over town for you!"

"Obviously not *all* over town."

"Look, you can't do that. I am trying to run a business here."

"Okay, I will never do it again." Roscoe chuckled to himself because that was awesome!

The tour bus was completely loaded, and when Roscoe stepped on, the driver released the air brakes with a loud hiss and the bus lurched forward. He needed a shower but that would have to wait.

"Okay, gather around," Nate said.

Everybody knew what this was about, as the very rotund man lowered himself into a seat.

"Look, all you guys have got to be careful. If you get a chick pregnant, your career will probably be over and then it will be on your back the rest of your life."

The band snickered as all of them knew who he was talking to. They also knew that Nate probably was not speaking from experience. The big man was breathing hard as his anger built up and his voice became high-pitched. Nate had no kids, so he didn't know what he was doing when it came to children, and a sixteen-year-old was even more complicated. He thought you were supposed to raise your voice until you were shouting but that was useless. And spanking was not an option because Roscoe could undoubtedly kick his ass. At the end of the tirade, everyone was laughing because they couldn't hold it back any longer, and this was a way for everyone to establish the pecking order in the band.

Nate stomped to the back of the bus to pout. Roscoe, on the other hand, was on cloud nine and thought he was the best lover on the planet. Becky's response during their tryst made him miss her almost immediately after leaving, but he dreamed of the future, and he thought for a second that he could get her to join him in another town. But as the bus ride continued for hours, he began to realize the reality of the situation. He then realized that he would never see her again.

Oh well, there will be thousands of girls on this tour, he thought.

CHAPTER 5

2005

The nurse in the ER did all the standard evaluations such as blood pressure, pulse, respirations, and alertness. His level of consciousness which in this case was very questionable. The nurse drew four tubes of blood so they could test his blood alcohol level. After that, they started administering three medications. The medications were D50 to treat hypoglycemia, thiamine to help the body process glucose, and of course, Narcan to reverse the effects of narcotics. This combination of drugs was common in referred to as the cocktail.

Katie left him snuggled up in his Bear Hugger blanket, and she went to another room to take care of another one of her patients. When she had a chance, she contacted the psychologist on duty for the hospital. Roscoe was snoring like a baby when she left.

"Hi, John. This is Katie Jennings in the ER."

"Hi, Katie. What's going on in your neck of the woods?"

"John, I have an elderly man in the ER. He is A and O times one, and I have taken all the standard steps. He doesn't seem to be on drugs, and we have done all the tests that we could think of. He is not responding to 'the cocktail.' He doesn't seem to be hypothermic. And we need an evaluation as soon as possible."

"Well, let's take a step back, Katie. So his orientation is to self only, and there is no response to dextrose, thiamine, and Narcan. Does he seem to have any recognizable mental challenges?"

"Not that anyone here can notice."

"Well, since he is in the ER, and he appears to be stable, we have some time."

"That's true," she said.

Roscoe stayed in the ER for twelve hours, the ER doctor did all the tests he could think of. Finally, he turned the case over to an internist who was on call. The internist admitted him to the to the hospital. A nurse aide rolled the elderly man down to the medical floor of the hospital. As Roscoe felt the movement of the bed rolling down the hallway, he said. "Mom?"

The nurse aide looked around and responded, "No, not your mom, sir. It's just me."

"Where's Mom?"

"I don't know where your mom is, sir."

The nurse aide finished the trip to room 205 and a nurse followed them into the room. They transferred the man over to the hospital bed and then things started happening. Roscoe had traded one foreign environment for an even fancier foreign environment. There were lots of beeps, a blood pressure cuff inflating as well as a few people talking in a strange language. Then Brenda, the floor nurse helped the aide get the ER bed out of the room. It was daylight outside, and Roscoe watched the clouds rolling by in the sky.

She walked around the bed and put the bars up which prevented the patients from rolling out of the bed. He stared at the highly polished chrome bars on the sides of the bed. Roscoe laid in the bed and alternatively stared at his reflection in the chrome bars and tracked Brenda's movements with his eyes.

"What's your name, sir?"

Roscoe didn't speak, instead, shook his head back and forth.

"Okay, no worries, sir. We will get everything figured out for you."

"Where's Mom?"

"We will find her and let you know where she is. Okay, sir? In the meantime, what is your last name?"

"I'm sorry, but I have to go to the potty."

"You have to use the bathroom. Okay, let me disconnect a few things," Brenda said. She unplugged the EKG monitor and rolled the

IV stand while he walked with an uncertain gate. His open-air gown waved in the breeze. This was a much better option than letting him evacuate his bowels in the bed. She put a collection hat in the toilet so they could see how his bowels were functioning.

After Roscoe was moved to the first floor, John Daly cane down to his room to do a psychological evaluation.

"Hi, Roscoe," John said.

Roscoe watched him as he walked around the room and sat down in a chair at the foot of his bed. Roscoe's eyes had the look of fear in them.

"So, Roscoe, what do you do? Where do you work?"

Roscoe didn't say anything he just stared at him. Brenda watched the proceedings from the corner of the room. Then John noticed that Roscoe was tapping out a beat on the sheet that covered him. Since he was getting nowhere with the patient, he thought he would take a risk and bring up the musical beat that Roscoe was producing.

"Roscoe, what song are you playing?" John asked.

Roscoe let a small smile form on his lips. John saw that and knew he had an in with this patient.

"You know Roscoe, I like music too. Let's see, I like Mustang Sally. Have you ever heard that song?"

Roscoe stopped tapping and he sat there quietly. The smile grew slightly bigger.

"Mustang Sally," John sang out loud in the hospital room.

"Guess you better slow your Mustang down. Mustang Sally now baby, oh lord, guess you better slow your Mustang down," John belted out in his best Wilson Pickett imitation.

Roscoe began nodding as the song played in his mind. That's when the smile broke out on his face. Then the tapping began in earnest. And finally, Roscoe let a laugh escape. John knew he had achieved a breakthrough.

"So what's your full name, Roscoe?"

"Roscoe Gillette."

"Now, we are getting somewhere," John said, quickly jotting that that down. He handed the piece of paper to Brenda.

"Now you can register him into your system and would you do me a favor and contact Adult Protective Services and see if he is in their system."

"Sure, John," Brenda responded. As she left the room, she thought John had made a major breakthrough.

Wow, a song was the key factor in reaching this aging man. She wondered how old he was. Maybe this information was in the hospital computer system.

"So, Roscoe, do you play music?" John asked.

Roscoe smiled a broad smile.

"So I assume that is a yes?" John inquired.

Roscoe nodded his head.

"What kind of music do you play Roscoe?"

"All kinds," Roscoe said.

"Tell me another song that you like."

Roscoe pressed his fingers against his forehead just above his eyes.

"I don't know."

"Come on, you make me embarrass myself singing. But that's okay, you'll think of something."

"Where's Mom?"

"That's interesting, Roscoe. Tell me more about this, who is mom?"

Roscoe shook his head. Tears began running down his cheeks, and John knew that he had hit the mother lode. But he also knew that this guy's mind was so far gone that he was going to have to be a lot more creative to get to the bottom of the story. This seemed to be a typical case of dementia, and he thought it was caused by Alzheimer's. This disease often made John shake his head in amazement. It was a very cruel disease that took the most elemental aspects of a human being away from people. Among the things that people lose were the cognitive processes of the brain, or in other words, it was a basic brain-wasting disease.

"No record of him in the hospital computer, until right now," Brenda said.

"That's surprising," John said. "I thought he would be a frequent flyer."

"Maybe he forgot his real name," Brenda said, smiling.

"Or maybe he knows his real name but he doesn't want us to know it," John said, carefully watching for any reaction from Roscoe, but nothing came up.

"Time to get the polygraph out."

It was John's turn to chuckle.

"That won't be necessary," he said as he turned on his iPhone. He scanned down the list of songs from the sixties.

"We always get a good reaction from him with music."

"There seems to be more than a casual familiarity to these songs," Brenda said.

"I agree. It looks like he played these songs or something."

"He seems to have about twenty things that he keeps repeating."

"Like, 'Where's Mom?'"

"I wonder what the history of that is."

"Well, we can probably narrow it down to a couple things, either his mother left him or the mother of his child is somehow missing."

"I'll look in the phonebook and see if there are any relatives in this area," Brenda said.

"Good idea."

Brenda flipped through the phone book, "Let's see E… F… G… Goldberg, Grange, Griffin, Gillette."

There were six Gillettes in the phone book. Brenda called them and four answered and when asked if they knew someone by the name of Roscoe, they said no. Two of them didn't answer. She decided she would have to follow up later. Then she got Roscoe ready for bed, and he fell asleep quickly and easily.

The next day, Adult Protective Services came to the hospital to talk to John and discuss finances and the care of such a patient for a long-term stay, with no money forthcoming.

Brenda made a note for herself to finish calling the other two numbers the next day, and then she went to give report for the next shift.

* * *

When Liz pulled into the driveway of the house, she immediately saw the for sale sign. She walked down the very familiar driveway to the back yard. Salt hung heavy in the air and gulls flew overhead with their distinctive and lonesome cries. The gravel crunched and ground under her feet. The humidity was high today, and she felt the microscopic beads of sweat on her upper lip. As she finished her walk into the backyard, she wanted to turn around and run back to the car. It was as if a bad memory was pulling her forward into a memory that she never wanted to revisit. And she continued forward as if she could rewrite the past and change the outcome. She had lived in this house when she was twenty-two. That was twenty years ago.

Liz walked further down the yard until she could see the beach down below. The ocean extended out as far as she could see and the sun was about to breach the horizon. Tears ran down her face as she remembered the year that she turned twenty-five and found out that she was pregnant. Her child was a beautiful little girl with blond braids that she named Elise. Elise's father didn't stick around and when Elise was born, Liz was a single parent.

Liz looked through her tears at the beach that was as least two hundred feet below the backyard. The beach was a place that Liz never wanted to remember but knew that if she didn't deal with her demons, they would never let her rest.

Liz had taken Elise down to the beach that day seventeen years ago. Liz was tired from long night shifts at work, and when they got to the beach, they laid towels out and before long, she dozed off. When she woke up her, gorgeous girl was gone.

Now, it was a morning during a time that Liz had found herself back at the house of her nightmares. Suddenly, the sun broke the distant ocean and a green light flashed across the horizon.

CHAPTER 6

1970

Becky was despondent and she sat in the emergency room crying. Her anxiety was starting to build up again, but now she had the cruel realization that she may be alone for the rest of her life. She started hyperventilating again and quickly began exhaling into the bag again.

The bag was becoming damp and worn from her exhalations. Finally, the rescue breathing caused the bag to tear, and all she had left was a wet piece of brown paper. She balled the paper up and threw it across the room.

I can't even do this right, she thought.

A nurse walked in just at that moment.

"Did you wear that bag out?" she asked with a pleasant smile.

"Yeah, I'm a failure at everything," Becky said with a huge pouty lip.

"Well, I wouldn't say you failed. Paper bags will only last so long, so I would say that the bag failed."

"Why did he leave me?" Becky sputtered out.

"I'm sorry, why did who leave you?"

"My boyfriend!"

"I just came on shift, so I am not familiar with what was going on."

"I gave him everything."

"Oh, sweetie, I wouldn't get too upset. Guys are always doing that. You just have to pick yourself up by your boot straps and get back into the game."

"No, I'm never going to talk to that boy."

"Yeah that's what we all say," the nurse said, chuckling.

"But guys are such jerks."

"You are preaching to the choir, girlfriend."

"But I loved him!"

"How long were you two together?"

"Well, I just met him, but I have known about him for a long time."

"When you say you just met him, like a month ago?"

"No, last night."

"Seriously, forget about that guy. You are never going to see him again," the nurse said, shaking her head.

Becky burst out crying again.

"Here are some more paper bags. You are going to need them," the nurse said.

Meanwhile, there was a rodeo going on in town. Rodeo clowns are the people who distract the bulls while the cowboys escape. A rodeo clown named Lane Thism was doing his job of interference with the massive beast when a huge hoof came down. The worst part of the accident was that Lane's feet were side by side. The hoof got both of his feet, and while Lane was down in the dirt writhing in pain, the other clowns covered for him. They got the angry bull out of the arena, and an ambulance was called. Lane was rushed to the emergency room, and the doctors and nurses that were helping Becky were pulled away. The curtain was open because of the large crowd of people, and she watched as they cut away his jeans and started to cut his boots when he screamed.

"Nooo! These are my best boots!" Lane shouted.

"My name is Dr. Johnson, and we are going to cut these boots off because if you don't, you could potentially loose both your feet."

"Oh, shit. I just paid eighty dollars for those damn things, that is two weeks' pay!"

"Well, I will make straight cuts down the sides and then you can take them to a cobbler, and they will fix these for you."

Once the boots were off, the doctor tipped them over and a couple tablespoons of blood dripped out of each one. Lane was taken to X-ray immediately, and in addition to several toe fractures and one calcaneus fracture, his ankles were badly swollen, but there were no fractures to the ankles that were noted. After the X-rays were done, the doctor went to work. First, he did a bilateral matrixectomy to remove the shattered great toe nails. Then he put a cast around the foot with the calcaneus fracture.

Becky watched everything from her room, and then someone realized she had full view of all the action so they pulled the curtain on Lane's room. The show was over, but someone rolled a tray of surgical tools out of Lane's room.

The emergency department had gotten much busier, and a nurse came into Becky's room to see if she could move things along.

"So how are you feeling?"

"Much better."

"Are you feeling well enough to go home?"

"Yes, I will be fine."

"Okay. Well, here are your instructions, and you can get dressed in these disposable scrubs. Is there someone who can pick you up?"

"No, but I live pretty close, so I will be fine."

"Okay, well, good luck with all the men of this world. And if you can figure them out, let me know."

Becky left her room, and the staff was too busy with the chaos in the ER. She needed a plan to get over this disaster her life had become. As she passed the tray of medical tools, she reached over and picked up the two scalpels and then quickly walked out the door. She went to a bench by the emergency room entrance. Becky's mind was not equipped to deal with this loss. Now that she was out of the protective arms of the emergency department, she was unable to keep it together. Becky began to quiver and had no resources to deal with this and didn't know what would happen next. She looked at the two scalpels and decided she must take this next step to relieve her pain and stress. She was alone, and there was no one who could help her. She had never cut herself on purpose.

* * *

Roscoe sat up in bed and he tapped out a beat on his legs. John, with Adult Protective Services, was trying hard to find a placement for him, but he kept coming up with one road block after another. All the possibilities were full, and they were running out of options. Suddenly, Roscoe stopped his drum line and stared straight ahead. Slowly, his mouth began to form the words.

"Becky," he said slowly. "Mom," he mumbled. Both of them were barely whispers.

John came back into the room.

"Hi, Roscoe," he said.

Roscoe just nodded.

"So, Roscoe, I'm just wondering do you have any family in this area?"

Roscoe stared at him and shrugged his shoulders.

"Well, Roscoe, we may have found someone that you are related to. Her name is Elizabeth Gillette, and she lives in this town."

Roscoe shrugged his shoulders again.

"Okay, well, I am going to try and get in touch with her."

John went and found a phone book.

The phone in Liz's house rang once, twice, on the third ring, a gruff male voice came on the line.

"Hello?"

"I'm trying to reach Elizabeth Gillette."

"Who's calling?" a very challenging voice responded.

"My name is John, with Adult Protective Services, can I speak with Elizabeth?"

"Liz," the man shouted.

In about thirty seconds, a very demure, sweet voice came on the line.

"Hello, is this Elizabeth Gillette?"

"Who's calling please?"

"My name is John Daly, and I am with Adult Protective Services, here in…"

There was silence on the phone as Liz tried to put all of this together.

"Most people call me Liz."

"Oh, okay. Well, thank you, Liz."

"How can I help you, John?"

"Are you related to a Roscoe Gillette?"

Liz's face flushed and her throat tightened. She knew the name but had never met her father. Her mother had lost track of him shortly after Liz was born. Liz was hoping he had died a very painful death because he didn't seem to have any interest in Liz or her mother. Liz wasn't sure if he even knew that she existed. A lot of people from her mom's generation told her about her father and that she was the splitting image of her mother. And then there were the photos. She thought she was looking in a mirror when she looked at her mom's photos. Unfortunately, she was only ten when her mom died of pancreatic cancer. At the time, though, no one could find her father, and she started a life of foster care with many different families and in many different homes.

Liz didn't like the foster homes, and she had lost the majority of her identity. She didn't have a real clear idea of who she was or what she wanted out of this life. When she turned eighteen, she was released from the foster care program. She began working retail jobs just to pay her bills. Then one night, she went to a local karaoke contest and she left the crowd speechless. She was twenty years old, and a standing ovation shocked her to her roots. She started saving her pennies so she could take singing lessons. However, most of the people at the karaoke contest thought she had been singing for years, especially a producer who often came to these events looking for untapped talent. Liz did everything she could to keep from getting pregnant because the last thing she wanted was a life like her mother's.

* * *

Becky had been taken to the emergency room after the syncopal episode at the concert. Roscoe came by to visit her, and she fell into his dreamy eyes and smooth talk. She left the hospital with him, and they went to a hotel were they made love. Becky left the hotel room completely naked and very pissed off at Roscoe but at the same time, still deeply in love with her favorite singer.

She went out to a bench in front of the hospital and slit her wrists. She was terrified as the moment approached. But when the blade caused the skin to gape open and the blood first began to bead up and then flow, she was surprised that when the act happened, it was relatively painless, and for a second, Becky thought that may be because of adrenaline. Then it gave her a moment of peace, and she thought it would only take before she was released into the afterworld. Fortunately—or not—for Becky, an Emergency Medical Technician was restocking his ambulance, and he looked over to see blood flowing out of the girls wrists and a puddle forming under the bench.

Becky had managed to cut both wrists, and she was beginning to drift into unconsciousness. Parker Miths was a new EMT, and he had never seen uncontrollable bleeding like this, but he had studied emergency care in the brief course he had taken. He grabbed a pack of 4x4s, a couple of roller bandages, and a few triangular bandages. Then he ran over to the woman who had become wobbly as she sat on the bench.

Direct pressure, direct pressure, he thought. He had never seen lacerations like this before, and the only thing he could think of was covering the wounds, so he grabbed the pack of 4x4s and slapped them on each of her wrists. Once the injuries were out of sight, he was able to bring his heart rate back under control. He suddenly had a realization that blood directly out of the human body was odorless. He leaned his full body weight against the woman's arms and pressed them down into the concrete.

Now that he had done the first step, he thought he should treat for shock, but his hands were tied up, and he didn't want to release direct pressure. Basically, he needed help. Just then, two people walked out of the ER.

"Get a doctor!" he screamed hysterically.

They were confused, but they turned on their heels and ran back inside. Within a few minutes, the parking lot was swarming with doctors, nurses, and all manner of medical personnel. Someone produced a gurney, and they lifted the injured woman up unto it and wheeled her back whence she had come.

CHAPTER 7

2005

Eli Animas was in total control of his destiny. And no one was going to pull anything on him. He met Liz in a bar where she was singing and her boyfriend was giving her a lot of hassle about everything she was doing. When her boyfriend walked out to smoke, the imposing Eli went outside too. When the guy held the lighter up the end of his cigarette and his attention was temporarily diverted, Eli cold cocked him.

"You never talk to a woman like that!" Eli yelled at the semi-conscious man, and all his friends took off in different directions. Then he went back inside to claim the prize of his overbearing violence.

When her last set ended, Liz was packing up, and Eli walked up and tried to talk very sweet to her.

"That guy won't ever bother you again."

"What guy?" she replied.

"That guy with the spiky hair."

"Who, my boyfriend?" Liz said while blushing hard.

"If you say so."

"Well, what happened to him?"

"We had a disagreement out in the parking lot."

"Is he okay?"

"Well, if he has any brains he would be in the hospital right now."

"Why did you send him to the hospital?"

"Because he was giving you a rash of shit while you were working, and you just don't treat a lady like that."

"He always does that. That's my boyfriend," she said with a sheepish grin.

"Well, why don't you go out with me, and I will show you how you should be treated."

Liz had been thinking that she wasn't treated that well recently, but she knew she needed help to leave this very aggressive guy.

Maybe this would be my ticket out, Liz thought. She reached up and touched her left eye causing a little bit of pain. She had some makeup over her, eye and she worried that her disguise was failing.

"Ah, yeah. We can try that," she said as she looked around to make sure they weren't being watched.

"I will make you the happiest girl in this town."

"But you have to be careful with my boyfriend. He is really mean."

"Your *ex*-boyfriend is no problem. I could squash him like a bug."

Liz gazed at his biceps stretching the T-shirt sleeves that he was wearing, and she should have realized right there that she was going from the pot to the frying pan. Liz had a really bad habit of picking the wrong guys. And unfortunately, that pattern was going to continue.

Eli moved in with Liz because his ex-girlfriend had a restraining order against him. The courts put the muscle behind that order and the threat of jail time solidified it. Liz's boyfriend came by her house a couple times to apologize, and on at least one occasion, went to the hospital to get a broken arm set in a cast.

For the first year, Eli was able to keep his anger under control whenever he was around Liz. But in private, he did some damage. Whenever Liz wouldn't acquiesce to his demands, he grabbed her around her arm, and she couldn't free herself from the vice-like grip. Then he threw her into the refrigerator. She ended up with five bruises on the bicep of her right arm.

"You never disobey me!" Eli screamed. "I'll teach you the penalties for disobeying me."

"And you will spend the rest of your life in prison!"

"We will see about that."

The next day, he was apologizing endlessly for his behavior. The ebb and flow of an abuser's mood swings was studied by psychologists since the dawn of man. That was followed by a month of good behavior on Eli's part. Then he snapped again, and Liz had to dig out the bruise concealing make-up. Liz had a very difficult time walking away from guys like Eli. It was her need to be accepted that made her put up with the abuse. And she got good at covering the bruises and making up stories for the emergency room staff.

"Eli, what do you think I should do about my father?" Liz asked.

"What do you mean, what should you do?" Eli responded. "Forget about the bastard."

"I know but he is the only blood I have in this world."

"Yeah, but he doesn't even know you exist."

"Well, you don't know that."

Eli stopped and began thinking, which was a chore for the man to do. *This guy could be worth millions and Liz could inherit everything*, he thought.

Suddenly, his tone changed completely. "Well, maybe you should meet him and just see how it goes, but I want to be there."

"Why do you need to be there?"

"Just to make sure you are safe."

"He's an old man!"

"Can't be too careful," Eli said, and he turned to conceal a grin.

"Okay, well, let's go to the hospital and meet with this guy named John."

Two days later they walked into John Daly's office in Memorial Hospital.

"Hi, Mr. Daly," Liz said, as she tapped lightly on the door.

"Come in," John said.

"I am Liz Gillette, and this is my boyfriend, Eli."

Eli had an almost permanent scowl on his face and when he shook hands, he tried to make the recipient of the handshake squirm, but John Daly just looked at him and smiled.

THE GATE WAS OPEN

"Eli. That's a good Irish name. And that's a very firm handshake you have, sir."

Eli just looked at him and shrugged.

"Sit down," John said.

"So I think I should start by saying that I have never met my father."

"That you know of," John interjected.

"Well yes, at least not in the formative part of my life. And I am not very comfortable meeting him."

"I totally understand, but it might not matter if you had ever met him."

"What the hell does that mean?"

John looked at the big brute of a man. "What that means is Mr. Gillette has a pretty convincing case of Alzheimer's."

"Alz—what?" Eli said. "Why don't you speak English?"

"Eli, let the man talk!"

Eli sat there and sulked.

"My apologies, Mr. Daly. I don't speak medical terminology," Liz spoke up to diffuse the situation.

"Alzheimer's is a degenerative brain disease. To put it in simple terms, your dad had lost most of his mental facilities. So he may not remember you, even if he knew you well."

"Really? So do you do tests to determine this?"

"We don't need to. When you meet him, you will see there is not much left."

"So what can we do?" she asked.

"Well, there are no places to put him, and the senior residences and memory care units are all full. So I was hoping that you could take him in and house him and take care of him."

"Oh, hell no," Eli shouted.

"Eli, please. He's not your father; he's mine."

Eli made a steely look at his girlfriend, but he bit his lip, and he also knew that he would be cut out of the take if he wasn't careful.

"So how will I be really sure that this is my father?" Liz asked.

"Probably the only way to do that is a DNA test," John answered.

"I don't know. It's just that I have never met this man."

"Well, baby, you should take the test. Just so that you know," Eli said, trying to turn her doubts into a money-making decision.

John didn't like this guy, and he wished he could say something that would put the power into her court. But the problem was that she had no strength in her convictions, especially in the face of such a bully.

"Well, why don't you meet Roscoe, and maybe that will help you make a decision."

"Okay," she said.

Eli was obviously clueless what this might mean. Roscoe would be living with them and he mostly was focusing on a big payday.

The three of them walked into the medical floor of the hospital. They found their way to Roscoe's room, and John knocked on the door. No response came from the inside of the room. John opened the door a crack and spoke.

"Roscoe?"

There was a rustling of the sheets, and not wanting Roscoe to walk to the door, he poked his head in.

"Roscoe, I have some folks that want to meet you," John said.

Roscoe nodded a little, and John swung the door open. The three of them strolled into the room and stood in front of Roscoe's bed.

"Hi, Roscoe," John said. "Thank you for seeing us."

Roscoe's eyes scanned the faces in front of him he saw John's kind face and then he winced a little when he landed on Eli's face. Then he got to Liz's face. He froze there and was locked onto her gaze.

"Mom?" he said in a quiet whisper of a voice.

Liz was stunned, her mouth dropped open and she returned the quiet stare. This standoff went on for at least a minute, then the silence was broken by Eli.

"Well, Jesus, why don't you two take a picture, they last longer." He chuckled in a goofy way which showed that he was uncomfortable with the silence.

Then John interjected, "Roscoe, do you know these people?"

"Mom," came the pronouncement with the loss of the questioning inflection this time.

Liz appeared a little uncomfortable.

"I'm sorry, sir, but I don't have any children," she said, then remembering his age, she realized that was a silly statement.

"Mom," Roscoe said even louder this time.

"Damn, this guy's a freak!" Eli said.

"John, does he understand what I am saying," Liz asked.

"It's hard to say. He's been saying that to everyone since he was found."

"Oh, so it is just a comment. It doesn't mean he recognizes anyone," she said.

"Yes, but I was watching his eyes, and this time, they had a look of familiarity to them."

"But we have never met," she said with frustration in her voice.

"Well, who knows? maybe you've ran into each other at some point in the past."

"Yeah, but he thinks I am his mother."

"What a weirdo," Eli said.

"Sir, I'm sorry, but that's not helping things here. Would you be more comfortable waiting in the hallway?"

"The hell with you, dude, I have as much right to be here as anyone," Eli said in a very gruff tone.

"Why don't you go down to the cafeteria and get us some coffee," Liz said.

"Damn it, that's bullshit!" Eli said as he stormed out of the room.

Liz sat down on the bed next to Roscoe.

"Hi, Roscoe. We have the same last name, so I am wondering if we know each other?"

"Mom," his face lit up as he said it even louder.

CHAPTER 8

1970

Becky was in trouble. Not only did she just escape death, but also she was about to embark on a life of constant and unremitting evaluations of her mental health. Even average members of the public and family members would start every interaction with, "How are you doing?" And when she would say she was doing fine, "Really?" would be the follow up.

It would eventually drive her crazy, if she wasn't already there.

But first, the emergency room staff had to save her life. The scalpels were very sharp, and her adrenaline was pumping into her body at the highest level when she put the very sharp instruments up to her wrists. Becky wanted to end her life quickly so she wouldn't suffer, so she pushed the blades down with a lot of force. She cut through fascia, ligaments, blood vessels and nerves. Basically, what doctors were faced with were two hands barely attached to the arms. They were hanging on by a thread.

The doctors gathered together to discuss this case. The emergency room doctor said that the only recourse in this case was to finish the job and amputate the hands. However, a surgeon who was experienced with reattaching severed limbs argued that there was a chance that he could save the hands, mostly because the time of injury was minimal, having happened right outside the ER. Tourniquets were applied to both arms immediately, thus limiting blood loss. Luckily, two surgeons could work on the patient with her arms stretched out in a T configuration. A separate team worked on each side to minimize the time the patient had to be kept under anesthesia. It was a step-by-step process for the surgeon—he would find a blood vessel or nerve and then he would search for the connecting end. Often times, the blood vessels would retract back into the limb when they were severed.

The reattachment of both hands took a little over five hours. The procedure was fatiguing and toward the end of the procedure, the doctors were applying all kinds of ways to stay awake. Throughout the procedure, the doctors had several pints of O-negative blood running to replace the blood that was sitting on the pavement under the bench outside the emergency department. The lab was called, and before the surgery started, they drew a few tubes of blood.

Five hours later her hands were reattached, and within minutes, they both flushed pink again as the blood flow was restored. But this was just the beginning of her challenges, a couple of the doctors wondered if she had the mental fortitude to deal with these challenges. If she wanted to end her life, then the slightest difficulty might just put her over the edge again.

Why did we work this hard on someone that might just end it all? Oh well, they thought, *it was good practice.*

It would take Becky a lot of time to get function back to her hands, because even though the nerves were attached, it would take almost two years for them to heal completely and for function to be restored. The surgery staff congratulated themselves when they saw all the positive signs of the surgery.

After surgery, the breathing tube was removed from Becky's trachea, and she was taken to recovery to make sure there were no problems from the long time on anesthesia. Then she was rolled down to her room where she would spend the next couple of weeks to heal. She had to be sedated on numerous occasions because the surgeries were so fragile that too much movement would damage them. When Becky woke up, her hands were still numb and she was still a little dizzy from the extreme loss of blood. The doctors that were involved in the surgeries would visit her. Her hands were so wrapped up in bandages she looked like a boxer.

And of course, because this was a suicide attempt, a psychologist came in also.

"Hello, Rebecca," the older man with a full white beard said. His glasses were perched at the end of his nose.

"Hello," Rebecca said in a muted groggy voice.

"How are you feeling today?" he said with a gruff tone.

Becky always thought that was a required question. She had just tried to kill herself and her hands were barely attached to her arms.

"Oh, I am doing just great!" she said with a tone of condemnation.

The old man chuckled and then said. "I apologize, Becky." Then the man arranged his paperwork. "I'm Dr. Samuelson, and I'm a psychologist."

"I figured they would send in a shrink!"

"Actually, we stopped shrinking heads years ago."

"Very funny."

"Thank you. I've been working on my one-liners."

"I can't believe they call you a doctor."

"Well, most people call me the cook."

"Wow, I want to blow my brains out, and you are making this look like a comedy act."

"No, but sometimes laughter is the best medicine."

"Laughter? Are you insane!"

"Some people think that, but I refute that with every breath I take."

"Okay, well, one thing's for sure, you haven't taken my mind off my problems."

"Good, now let's get serious."

"Oh damn, just when I was having fun," Becky quipped.

"Haha. Well, that's one thing I am sure you have not taken into consideration."

"Oh, trust me, I have considered everything."

The doctor paused and looked down at the paperwork in his hands.

"I have your lab results here."

"Do they have a lab test for crazy?"

"You are pregnant."

She froze in midsentence. Then she locked her stare on the doctor.

"You have got to quit the jokes, dude!"

"This is the serious stuff, Becky."

"What?"

"Yes, ma'am. When they drew your blood, they ordered an HCG and that came back positive. You are pregnant."

"What?"

The doctor just sat there and stared at her.

"This should be the good news, Becky. Most women are elated by this news."

"Look at me you, fool! I just cut my hands off, and I still can't feel them."

"Yes, but the doctors did an incredible job reattaching your hands, and it will take a long time for you to get the feeling back, but eventually, it will return."

"What?"

"Sorry, Becky."

"How am I going to pick up a baby?"

"As I said, eventually your control and sensation will return to normal."

"But I can't be a mother right now!"

"Lots of women start motherhood at earlier ages. It will make you grow up really fast."

"Damn it. How could this happen?"

"I think you know the answer to that question," Dr. Samuelson replied.

"Fuck!"

"Yeah, you got it."

"Would you get out of my room?"

"Of course," Dr. Samuelson replied, then he stood up and walked out of the room. He walked down to the nurses' station and approached the head nurse.

"We will have to put suicide precautions on that patient."

"She already has suicide precautions," the nurse replied.

"Yes, and if necessary, the precautions need to be redoubled."

"Okay, Doctor," the nurse said but thought, *I don't know what else we could do, if she really wants to die, eventually she will succeed.*

The next day, Becky woke up. She is still unable to use her hands.

"Nurse, nurse! she screamed.

The nurses rushed into her room.

"What's wrong?" the head nurse asked.

"I need an abortion!"

"You know, Becky, just give this some time. You will grow to love this life that is forming inside of you."

"No, I don't want this bastard child of that asshole."

"Who is the father?"

"Roscoe Gillette!" she screamed.

"You mean the musician?"

"Yeah!"

"Are you sure?"

"What do you mean, am I sure? I think I was there!" Becky retorted.

"Okay, Becky, just relax a little."

"Relax?" she screamed, then she started crying. Then she reached down and caressed her stomach. This was still early in her pregnancy, and she couldn't feel any movement.

Becky's mind had wild thoughts about aborting the fetus. She also thought about a life of raising a child. Of course, there was nothing she could do about it now. She was trapped in this hospital and she couldn't do anything about this because her hands were useless. In other words, her hands were tied.

CHAPTER 9

1970

As the bus pulled out of Willington, North Carolina, and eventually headed west to I-95, the band settled in, then the bus turned south. The rising sun was on their left, and Roscoe pulled the blind down because he was tired. The night before was a wild one, he couldn't believe how good that had felt. But now Roscoe just wanted to get some sleep. Nate was pacing up and down the center isle of the bus. Every time he passed Roscoe's seat, he was biting his lip and wondering if Roscoe could possibly be conscious for the concert tonight.

The bus rolled into Orlando at 6:00 p.m., and the bus stopped at a restaurant. Nate ordered a couple pots of coffee. The band ordered dinner and started drinking coffee. The concert that night wasn't great; in fact, Roscoe was down on everything. He even forgot the words for several songs and he ended up just saying, "La la la la," and sometimes just hummed his way through it. Eventually, the crowd caught on to this deception and the booing started. The rest of the band knew something was going on, and they tried to cover for him with distractive cords and one of the band members started singing for him. However, it was mostly a disaster, and people started walking out and demanding their money back.

The band came to a decision and walked backstage to discuss this problem. When they got backstage, the band members demanded an answer. Nate was infuriated and came storming through the door as only a three-hundred-pound man could.

"What the hell are you doing, Roscoe?" Nate yelled.

"I'm sorry, you asshole," Roscoe shouted.

"I'm trying to cover everyone's paycheck."

"I said I'm sorry!"

Roscoe got up and walked out of the auditorium. Nate panicked and tried to keep up with him, but the overweight man had knee pain and running was not in his repertoire. Roscoe slammed the door of the auditorium as he ran out. There were a group of young girls walking through the parking lot, and they turned when they heard the door slam. Roscoe had the same purple blazer on that he had onstage.

"Oh my god, it's Roscoe Gillette!" one of the girls screamed as she grabbed onto the arm of another girl. The girl that screamed was hyperventilating. The crowd of girls hesitated, and then one of them started walking over to Roscoe, holding out a concert program.

"Roscoe, will you sign this program for me please, please? I love you!"

The rest of the girls ran over to the first girl and hung on her shoulders with their mouths wide.

"Oh my god, I can't believe this is happening!"

Roscoe was in a state of unresponsiveness as he tried to shake off his anger. He didn't even know the girls were there at first. Then he snapped back to reality, and he realized he was in a group of adoring fans. He suddenly thought his dreams were coming true. All the girls were in the same class in high school, and they idolized Roscoe Gillette.

"Hey, can you girls give me a ride?"

Just hearing him speak the girls lost it, and the screams started anew. And then they just stood there speechless. He looked at them again and no one responded.

"Is that a no or a yes?" he inquired.

"Yes, yes! Yes, we'll give you a ride!" they yelled. Two of the girls were jumping up and down. None of them thought it was odd that their idol was who was playing on the stage a minute ago was now in their car. Roscoe was in the back seat with three girls. It was a tight fit, but no one really had a complaint.

"Where do you want to go?" the driver asked.

"Wherever you want to go," Roscoe said.

Nate got the band together and said they were going to finish the concert. Nate was an accomplished pianist, and he would take over for Roscoe. The rest of the group shook their heads in annoyance because of the audacity of that little punk kid that was trying to ruin their livelihood.

"Bobby, you can sing the majority of the songs, can't you?"

"Yeah, I can sing like a lark!" the bass player said. "But there are a few songs that I don't know."

Nate handed him a play list. "Cross off the ones you can't sing."

Bobby put a line through the ones he couldn't remember. Nate then adjusted the lists for the rest of the band.

When the band got back to the stage, the crowd eventually realized the star of the Backdoor Brothers was missing and started booing.

Meanwhile, Roscoe asked the girls too take him to a hotel.

"Well, there is a hotel right down the street," the driver said.

"That would be great!" Roscoe said.

When they arrived at the hotel, Roscoe said, "You ladies like to party?"

Like most young people, these ladies wanted to be part of the crowd.

"Of course, we party," one of the girls in the back seat said.

When they got to the hotel, Roscoe stepped out of the car and looked at the girls. Then he pointed at the sixteen-year-old driver and said, "You look the oldest of any of us. So why don't you go into the liquor store and get us a bottle of Jack?"

They got back into the car and drove to the liquor store.

Jamie was the driver, and she didn't like whiskey that much and decided to get a bottle of wine as well. She walked up to the counter with the two bottles of alcohol. She was trying to avoid eye contact with the cashier, but he was experienced at this and he decided to card her.

"Ma'am, I'm going to need to see your ID," he said.

"Oh, I left my wallet in the car," Jamie said.

"I'm sorry, but I can't sell to anyone underage."

"I know I look young, but I am thirty and I have a kid! And I am picking up some last minute supplies for a party."

The cashier was trying to watch her eyes, and he could tell the woman was trying to be deceptive.

"Could you just run out to your car and get your ID so I don't lose my job?"

"Fine," she shouted and walked out.

She got back to the car empty-handed, and the rest of the car moaned.

"Sorry, the guy was on to me," she said.

"Well, let's go to a bar. If the bartenders are busy, they will give us the drinks just to keep things moving," Roscoe said.

They got to the Highway Bar and Jamie said, "We can't so in as a group, so Roscoe and I will walk in and then you gals come in one or two at a time. I will need some more money to buy the shots, so every has to donate."

The girls handed Jamie fives and tens, and she got out and walked hand-in-hand with Roscoe into the bar. Roscoe pulled a hat down over his head which cast a shadow across his face. Over the next thirty minutes, the six of them were sitting at a table, and Jamie would walk up to different bartenders and got wine, whisky, and tequila shots. Roscoe started pushing the booze on every one at the table, and when anyone slowed down he would humiliate them until they threw back a shot.

Eventually, a couple of the girls went out to the dance floor and were trying to stay vertical until one of them face-planted onto the floor. The bouncers were notified and came over to the six drunk kids and kicked them out. By that time, it was too late; their fate was sealed.

The kids climbed back into the car giggling, one of them with a bad headache. Another one of the girls vomited a few times in the parking lot. Jamie had a bad feeling about this as she climbed into the driver's seat. But the alcohol tempered the foreboding she was feeling and she concentrated on finding the right key to start the car. She buckled the seatbelt because of the premonitions that were swirling around her brain. Kandace had a headache and climbed into the passenger's seat and fell asleep almost immediately. No one noticed the seatbelt that hung limp at her side. But back in the sixties, seat belts were not so revered. The four people in the back seat also ignored their seat belts because with that many people in one seat, it was impossible to dig them out and find one for each person. Roscoe is in the middle of the four people, and they were wedged in tightly.

As they left the bar, Jamie struggled to operate the vehicle and remember where she was driving. Then suddenly, sleep started creeping up into her brain. She thought it would be safer to take a side road instead of the interstate. As she drove down the road, the car became quiet as people were either drunk or asleep. Jamie was relying on some chatter, but now all was quiet. It was 1:00 a.m. The road went around a bend to the left. At that exact moment, Jamie's eyes drifted shut. The car continued straight, and there were no guardrails to change the trajectory of the speeding vehicle.

An oak seed had been carried by the wind to this exact spot, but that was fifty years before. It landed and rooted, and years later a road was put in right next to the tree, and from that moment on, the road channeled rain water to the tree roots. The tree thrived, and in the fifty years since the seed took root there, it grew to a massive size. When Jamie's eyes closed, the car barreled off the road and plowed into the tree which was like a concrete column.

The front end of the car crumpled, and the engine was shoved back into the driver's seat. The hot engine both burned and fractured Jamie's legs. Kandace, who was sleeping in the front passenger seat, was thrown upward and forward. The upper edge of the windshield where it attached to the roof scalped her and fractured her skull, causing a massive bleed to start. The blood started putting pressure on the brain as the skull which was supposed to protect the brain now caused the most damage.

There were no airbags at that time, so seat belts were the only chance for survival. The four people in the back seat were thrown forward in a very violent manner much like they had been grabbed by a massive animal and dropped in a jumbled heap. The smell of burning flesh permeated the scene of the accident from the very hot engine block sitting on Jamie's legs. This also cauterized the wounds and prevented Jamie from bleeding to death.

    Roscoe hit his head on the headrest for the front seat. Luckily, the head rest was padded. He was still conscious but very dizzy and not sure where he was. As he extricated himself from the car and the tangle of bodies, he felt a sticky substance on everything he touched. But he was unable to focus on anything, he just looked around trying to get his bearings. He heard a couple of girls whining beside him as everyone began to understand what had just happened.

CHAPTER 10

2005

Eli was pissed. He knew this guy had a boatload of money, and he didn't like being cut out of the discussions. He knew that Liz didn't have the spine to stand up for herself. Eli was worried that if she inherited a bunch of cash, she might donate to some charity. He hurried down to the cafeteria and grabbed an empty cup so he could at least make an appearance of getting coffee.

When he got back to the room, he both tapped on the door and walked in. He had a very controlling way about him. Liz and John were busy discussing the details of Roscoe's issues.

"Man, that coffee was good," Eli said when he walked into the room.

"Did you get me some?" Liz asked with a pout on her lips.

"Oh, I didn't know you wanted any," Eli said with a grin on his face.

"Don't worry, sweetie. I'm fine."

"So what did you guys decide?"

"I am going to the lab to get some blood drawn, so they can do a DNA test."

"Oh," Eli said.

"It is the only way we can be sure this is Liz's father," John said.

"Okay," Eli said, seeing the cash register adding up.

"Yeah, so if this is Liz's dad, I have told her that there is no room in the senior residence or the nursing home," John said.

"So if this is a match then I am considering taking him home with us," Liz mentioned and looked a little demure as the words came out.

"Ah well, we will see about that."

"But, Eli, if it's my dad, it is my only family."

"Well, we are family. We have been together for six months!" Eli said with a chuckle.

Liz just glanced at John to bolster her courage.

"Okay. Well, we'll see," she responded.

"But neither of us are nurses or doctors, so how the hell are we going to take care of someone who needs medical care?"

"Well, that is what John and I were talking about."

"And what was that?" Eli inquired.

"Roscoe can take care of his physical needs, but he needs someone to make the important decisions for him. In other words, he could live another ten years," John responded.

"But, honey, if he gets sick we don't have the money to take care of him."

"That was another thing that we were talking about," Liz replied and looked at John.

"Well, is it okay to discuss this at this time?" John asked Liz.

"Go ahead."

Eli had a stunned look on his face like they were discussing things behind his back.

"Well, Mr. Gillette has enough money to take care of himself for probably ten years."

"What?" Eli said as a smile began to grow across his face.

"But we have to be careful with that money because now we have three mouths to feed," she said.

Eli nodded his head as he pictured the big black Hemi diesel truck that he had been drooling over.

"But now we have to discuss something else," John said.

Liz just nodded her head.

"There is no cure for Alzheimer's disease. So if this is your dad, he will never get any better. And he may need hospitalizations from time to time."

"I will do my best to take care of him," she said.
"But you have to decide on his DNR status."
"Could you explain that?" Liz asked.
"DNR is an acronym for Do Not Resuscitate."
Liz had tears welling up in her eyes as the words hit her ears.
"So you mean you will just let him die?"
Eli was nodding vigorously.
"Yes, if his heart stops, we could respond with a full out cardiac resuscitation or we could let him go to the great beyond."
"I don't think I can make that decision. That would be like playing god." She sobbed.
"Oh, come on, Liz. Pull it together," Eli retorted.
"Well, we are way ahead of ourselves. I wanted you to start thinking this through, but let's get the DNA test first."

They all left the room, but not before Liz took one long look at Roscoe. He formed one word with his mouth: *Mom*. As she walked down the hallway she was haunted by this interaction.

Liz walked down to the lab with Eli by her side. He wanted to talk but she said nothing. When they got to the lab, she registered and then she was escorted into to another room and Eli never left her. He was afraid he would miss something. She rolled up her sleeve and then the phlebotomist tied a tourniquet around her arm. There was one problem, much like her mother, Liz had very small spidery veins. They were very small, and the first two techs missed the vein and didn't get any blood. Liz was running out of sight, so they called for a veteran of the lab with experience of getting blood from all kinds of veins, even invisible ones.

She started by palpating several areas that were common for drawing blood. Her finger tips were very sensitive and could feel an engorged vein deep under the skin. She selected a vein that was often overlooked in the wrist and commonly called the intern vein. It was in the wrist, and a lot of people went for the antecubital space in the elbow first. The phlebotomist started tapping Liz's wrist lightly, and within thirty seconds, the light blue vein began to reveal itself. The technician selected the smallest butterfly needle, which was usually reserved for children, and then with a deft touch, she slid the needle under the skin. Nothing. No blood return. She withdrew the needle slightly and then advanced it again with a slightly deeper angle. Nothing. Undeterred, she made one more attempt. Eureka. Blood started flowing into the vacuum tube until it was full. Because of the difficulty of getting this blood and the potential of the results, Liz felt her forehead sweating and she was a little lightheaded. Lights out.

Eli ran over and was shouting. "What did you do? Did you kill her?"

"No, sir. she just had a syncopal episode."

"What?"

"She just passed out, probably from the sight of blood," the experienced nurse said. "She will come around in a minute."

The nurse cracked a small vial under Liz's nose. The ammonia smelling salts did the job. Eli was leaning over her, and when she came back to consciousness, she was startled, maybe by his lethal breath. Her hand shot out, and she landed a punch squarely on Eli's nose.

"What the fuck!" Eli shouted.

His nose immediately started gushing.

"Sir, there is no reason to use that language in here."

"Damn, this is one disaster after another one!"

"Well, if you let your girlfriend beat you up, I'm sure that may affect your masculinity," the nurse said.

"Shut up, you bitch!" Eli shouted.

"Call security," the tech said.

When the security guard walked through the door, he saw a girl on the floor, a guy whose clothes were covered with blood, and blood all over the floor. The guy was plastering everyone with the vilest words in the English language, his eyes fixed on the security guard.

"This is the guy you sent to take care of me?" Eli blurted out.

The click of the handcuffs brought Liz back to consciousness.

"What happened?" she said.

"What happened?" Eli shouted.

Liz brought her arms up over her head, which was a visceral reaction she had like waking up from a deep sleep into a very violent place.

"What happened? What did I do?" Liz barely muttered out.

"Sir, if you want to stay here, you better shut your mouth," the security guard said.

"Eli, what's going on?" Liz said as she started to get her head back and saw the blood on the floor, especially pouring out of his nose.

The phlebotomist approached with two tampons in her hand.

"You are getting blood all over the lab, and you look like a fool. These will help stop the bleeding," the tech said.

"Yeah, well, how am I going to put those in with my hands cuffed?"

The tech walked up to him and firmly shoved the tampons into each naris. Now he looked like a walrus with two white teeth jutting out of his nose. The nurses and security guard couldn't help but chuckle.

"You piece of shit," he said to anyone in ear shot.

"One more word out of you, and I am going to call the cops and let them deal with you."

Eli was flexing his muscles against the handcuffs. His jaw was tense and the muscles there flexed and relaxed uncontrollably.

When Liz hit the floor, her tortoiseshell glasses went flying across the tiles. A lab tech picked them up and as a security guard lifted her and helped her into a bed, the tech put her glasses on a table beside the bed. Eli could taste the blood which was draining down the back of his nose. As he wriggled his nose from side to side, he could hear the click of a fracture and feel a small amount of pain that he would never admit to. But mostly, he felt humiliated because his petite, hundred-pound girlfriend broke his nose.

After all the excitement, Liz and Eli drove home. Eli just sat and simmered over the events of the last hour. Eli always drove because in the past, men always took control of a vehicle and the women rode as passengers. He had pulled the tampons out of his nose and a nurse bandaged his nose to secure the fracture. He couldn't stop shaking his head in disbelief and disgust.

Even though the accident happened when Liz was unconscious and she didn't even remember it, she apologized repeatedly. Eli pouted and he thought how different it would be if a guy had broken his nose and they weren't in a public place with a lot of witnesses.

CHAPTER 11

1970

Roscoe was out of the car, stumbling around, and he tripped and fell facedown on the street. Some bystanders tried to help him, but he unleashed a tirade of vulgarities and they backed off. Kandace was in the front passenger seat, and it seemed she was in a hurry to meet her maker. Jamie was cuddling a hot engine block, and the pain of second-degree burns was unbearable. She unleashed a gut-wrenching scream as the pain came from all corners of her broken body. She had third degree burns too but with that depth of burn the nerves are destroyed and the pain is reduced. The second-degree burns were the most bothersome, and she was trapped, so all she could do was verbalize her pain. The bleeding from bilateral femur and tibia fractures was somewhat reduced by the hot engine block. Unfortunately, the bleeding inside her thigh was not affected by the cauterizing effects of the hot engine block and continued unabated.

The smell of death hung heavy in the air along with the smell of antifreeze which was dripping down from the leaves of the oak tree. Kandace was close to death from a closed head injury. Jamie was dying from the array of fractures throughout her body. Roscoe struggled to stand up and then stumbled around in a daze. The other three girls had also extracted themselves from the backseat of the crumpled car. A crowd of bystanders had gathered and gawked at the carnage. One person had driven to a nearby town and called for an ambulance.

Some of the bystanders were trying to get Kandace out of the wreckage. Then the rescuers arrived, first in a 1950s fire apparatus, and then a Cadillac station wagon with a single rotating red light on the top pulled up. The bystanders had pulled Kandace's limp body out of the car. One of the ambulance attendants pulled the stretcher, and Kandace was carried over to the ambulance like a sack of potatoes. They plopped her down on the stretcher, and they lifted the whole apparatus up and rolled it into the ambulance. They shut the back door, and then both of the attendants jumped into the front seats and raced off to the hospital with basically a dying patient in the back. Kandace was left to save her own life and that looked doubtful.

After the ambulance left, the firefighters started working on Jamie. With hammers and pry bars, they attempted to separate her from the engine block which had essentially fused to her skin. Of course, the nylon pants she was wearing didn't help the situation. At one point, the pry bar put pressure against one of her fractures. The pain was cranked up to a point that she began to start dry heaves which led to a loss of consciousness. Eventually, they added a hacksaw to the work and a few strong men tore the driver's door into a hyperextended position. Then they slid the pry bar over Jamie's legs and under the engine block. Then they put their backs into it, and the heavy cast-iron block lifted an inch or two. They slid Jamie's limp body out of the driver's seat. As they did that, her legs were like a jumble of broken sticks. One of the fractures was compound, and the jagged end of the femur had a trickle of blood that dripped out of it, like a leaky faucet. The odor was so pervasive that one of the fire fighters couldn't handle it and walked away to vomit.

The rescuers were too busy to round up the other victims so bystanders took that task on. They managed to corral the remaining girls, especially the injured ones which weren't as mobile as the uninjured girls. One of the girls had a fractured arm, and the rest of the girls had various lacerations from flying glass and other objects that were loose in the car that became projectiles when the car melted into the tree.

Kandace had been thrown forward because she hadn't been wearing a seat belt. In addition to having a devastating closed head injury, her face hit the windshield and the glass was forced out. When her face hit the glass, it caused a laceration that completely circled her face. Essentially, her face was not attached to her skull anymore.

The firefighters were trained in putting out fires in the 1960s and they could splint fractures, but basic first aid was about the max of their medical experience. Triage was not a universally accepted technique in the sixties, and basically, the ambulance took the first person that they saw, and basically, the person that would least likely survive, no matter what was done in the ambulance or in the hospital.

When the ambulance rolled up to the emergency room, Kandace was basically dead on arrival. The only thing that was working was her heart and lungs.

However, the ER staff did everything they had been trained in. But there was no positive result, and they were basically just keeping the physical body alive. In the meantime, Jamie was also dying because she had been left at the scene, and she was the one that could have been saved by a quick transport to the hospital. By the time the ambulance returned to the scene, Jamie was as pale as a bedsheet. The same sequence that was done with Kandace was repeated. They gently lifted her limp, cold body and placed her on the blood-soaked stretcher. Although modern triage dates back to the 1700s, it had been refined a lot by the 1960s, but training in triage was intermittent, at best, until the 1980s, when the color-coded system of tags to classify levels of trauma appeared. Then a major push began to train everyone in a more logical approach to mass trauma incidents.

Kandace's brain was swelling from several arteries that had been torn in her brain. The doctor on duty that night recognized the signs of a closed head injury. He started preparing for another technique. Trepanning was another French technique that had come into play in the last few centuries. Trepanning was a method of reducing the pressure build up in the brain by drilling burr holes in the skull to allow excess blood to drain out, thus preventing excess pressure from building up and destroying Kandace's brain. But this was a last ditch effort and often did not work. For all intents and purposes, Kandace was brain dead and a ventilator was all that was keeping her alive.

An emergency room nurse pulled an ID card out of her pocket and then found her name in the phone book. Then she placed a call that everyone in the ER hated to do.

It was late in the night when the phone rang in the Jenkins home. Bill Jenkins was jolted out of an REM sequence. He was unsure of where he was for a second as he woke up.

"Mr. Jenkins?"

"Ah, yes."

"Mr. Jenkins, this is Nancy. I am a nurse in the emergency department."

"What?"

"Mr. Jenkins, do you have a daughter named Kandace?" the nurse asked.

"What?"

"Do you have a daughter named Kandace?" she said in an elevated tone.

Suddenly, Bill Jenkins snapped awake, and he was understanding the question.

"Yes. Yes, I have a daughter named Kandace."

His wife, Ethel, stirred in the bed beside him. "Bill, wake up. You are talking in your sleep again." She grabbed his arm and shook him.

Bill was fully awake now. "Honey," he said.

"What?" she said.

"Be quiet. Someone is on the phone…about Kandace."

"Mr. Jenkins, you need to come to the emergency department at Belle View Hospital, immediately."

"What's going on? What's wrong?"

"Kandace has been badly injured in a car accident."

Bill just stared with the phone to his ear. He didn't breathe. He tried to conceptualize what was being said and what was going on.

"Sir? Sir?" the nurse said.

"Yes," Bill shouted.

"Sir, you need to come to the hospital now. She was injured in a car accident."

"Okay, okay. I will be right there!" he said.

Then Bill let out a scream. "Nooo!"

"What are you doing? Are you having a nightmare?" Ethel asked.

"No! You need to get dressed!" Bill said, still shouting.

"What happened?"

"Kandace got hurt. She is in the hospital!" he said.

"Oh my god," she said.

Bill ripped his pajamas off and put his trousers on backward. Then he tore them off in a rage and grabbed a pair of swim trunks and pulled them over his boxers. Then they ran out of the house and got into the car. They drove at breakneck speed to get to the emergency department, as if that would have made a difference. All it did was put them at high risk of another vehicular accident. When they got to the ER, they were extremely hyper.

"Where is Kandace?"

"She is in the best hands that this hospital can offer. You will have to wait in the waiting room."

The nurses came over to him and said, "Sir, please don't shout in here."

The final burr hole was just completed and the surgeon inserted a pressure meter into the last burr hole. The smell of bone dust still lingered in the air. In the 1960s hyperventilation was one technique that was used to reduce the intracranial pressure. Kandace was intubated and the ventilator was set on a rate of thirty respirations per minute. The anesthesiologist kept an eye on the intracranial pressure meter to perfect the rate of respirations and reduce the pressure in her brain.

But despite his best efforts, the anesthesiologist noticed that gray matter was starting to squeeze out through the burr holes. A neurosurgeon was called in, and he came to the conclusion that a full trepanation of half of her skull would be the only thing that would save her life.

Then Jamie arrived by ambulance and was rolled into the emergency department. When she came through the doors of the ER, her skin tone was as pale as a bedsheet. A nurse put her index and middle fingers on Jamie's wrist, but could not find a pulse. Then she moved her fingers up to the carotid artery on the side of her neck. The pulse was barely detectable, and she could barely feel the rapid weak beating as Jamie just held on to life.

If the very hot engine block had not cauterized some of the wounds, Jamie would have bled out by now. But despite the life-saving effects of the heat, Jamie's left femur was fractured and had torn through nerves, muscle, and blood vessels, and the blood was flowing unabated. When she was brought into the emergency department, she was minutes from death. A very experienced ER doctor recognized the imminence of this event. Since Kandace had prepared the ER staff, they were ready for more injuries. The doctor had two fourteen-gauge intravenous lines flowing full bore. That action alone turned around the plunge down to the end of life as we know it, and Jamie held stable for a couple hours and then started the slow climb back up to the light that was life itself. Thirty minutes later, Jamie's parents were contacted, and a little while after that, they walked through the ER doors. While they were in the waiting room, three of Jamie's friends walked through the door with various injuries and were put into their rooms. Jamie's parents walked into one of the rooms.

"What happened?" they asked a girl with minor injuries.

"We got into an accident," she said.

"What did you hit?"

"Something very big and very hard," she said with her voice trembling. "I actually never saw what we hit but the car was completely destroyed."

"The car is gone?" Jamie's father shouted.

Then Jamie's father walked over to the wall and punched it, leaving a hole in the lath and plaster wall. But lath and plaster is not as fragile as modern-day sheet rock, and the man fractured two knuckles on his right hand.

"John, forget about the car. Jamie almost died!" her mother said with her voice quivering.

"Forget about the car? We don't have any money for another car!" her father shouted while massaging his sore fist.

CHAPTER 12

2005

When Liz and Eli got home from the hospital the day that the incident happened, Eli waited until they were alone in their house and the door closed before he grabbed her by both arms in a very tight squeeze, which she knew would leave some significant bruises.

"Eli, you are hurting me!"

"Look at my nose, Liz. It didn't hurt a bit, but you made a fool out of me around all those brainiacs."

"It was an accident."

"The next time you do anything like that, you might just wake up six feet under."

"But you know it was an accident."

"Well, next time, use your brain if you have one."

"I was unconscious, so let me go or I'm going to call the cops!"

He shoved her back as he released her arms. She fell backward and landed in a sitting position with her back against the kitchen cabinets. Then he shook his head and got control of himself.

Damn, I have to be cool until we find out about the old man's fortune, he thought. Then he was apologizing effusively.

"Baby, I'm sorry I grabbed your arms. Are you okay? Come here and sit down, and I will get you a beer."

Liz got up and walked into the bedroom and slammed the door behind her. Then she turned around and locked the door.

"Baby, you know I have always taken care of you ever since I saved you from that other guy that you were dating."

He knocked on the bedroom door. Then he tried the door knob and it was locked.

"Liz, come on let me help you out... Do you want anything?"

He realized he should just let it be or else he would be out of everything. Eli walked into the bathroom and turned on the light. Then he looked in the mirror and felt his anger starting to rise again. His nose had dried blood at the base of it and he could just barely make out a small hump on the bridge of his nose that he could see through the bandages. As he walked past the bedroom, he could hear her sobbing inside.

Oh well, she is crying all the time. She'll calm down by the morning, he thought. Then he flopped onto the couch for the night.

* * *

The hospital had a meeting about all the patients that were in their facility that were unable to pay. This was draining a lot of money from the hospital, and they discussed each patient and the possible resources that could help them.

The CEO was chairing the meeting and also at the meeting were the managers from the medical floor, the surgical floor, and the finance department as well as all the other specialties in the hospital.

"Okay, so we are going to start off with Mr. Roscoe Gillette," the CEO said.

"Yes, Mr. Gillette has been in our department for a week," the manager of the medical floor said.

"What are the costs so far?" the CEO inquired.

"He has run up a bill of just under one hundred thousand dollars," the financial person said.

"How old is he?" the CEO asked.

"Seventy-three," the medical floor manager said.

"Does he have Medicare or Medicaid?" he asked the financial person.

"We are looking into it," she responded.

"It looks like he has been living off his savings that he has accumulated."

"Well, why can't we access that?"

"Because you just can't go into a bank and say you want a hundred thousand dollars from someone's account. The person has to give you their permission, or give it to you."

"And Mr. Gillette probably can't understand that we want to get paid for taking care of him."

"Exactly," the medical floor manager said.

"What other sources of money might he have?"

"There is a woman that lives in town that came forward when we contacted her that might be his daughter."

"And is he her father?"

"She never knew her father, but she acquiesced to a DNA test."

"When will we know?"

"Friday."

"Okay, well then, we will find out on Friday if this person will take responsibility for him. Well, in the meantime, let's see if the nursing home in town will take him."

"We already checked. They are full; no vacancies."

"So we are committed till Friday, and we will meet on next Monday to discuss this further, okay?"

Everybody around the table nodded, and at that point, they moved to another patient.

* * *

When Eli woke up and staggered into the bathroom the next morning, he was shocked. Both of his eyes had an ecchymotic half circles under them.

"Damn, I am not going to wear makeup!" he choked out with his teeth gritted. Then he picked up his sunglasses and slid them on and looked in the mirror again and they covered most of the black eyes.

Liz came out of the bedroom with a bruise around each bicep. "Look at this," she said pointing to each bicep.

"Look at this," Eli countered pointing at his eyes.

"Oh, so I get bruises, too, because I accidentally broke your nose."

Eli shallowed hard and took a deep breath in an attempt to control his anger. Then he smiled a fake smile.

"I don't know what to say to you. Why don't we get some dinner tonight?"

"Oh, so that's it? You buy me dinner and I am supposed to forget about these bruises that you purposely left on me."

"Liz, every time this happens we go down the same road."

"You know, Eli, I apologize about a hundred times for a mistake, but you purposely injure me and you don't even know the words *I'm sorry*."

Eli got up and grabbed his sunglasses and stormed out the door.

For a week, Liz would go get food at restaurants and Eli would go to the bar. Eli would come home late every night and just crash on the couch. Then he would get up in the morning with a massive hangover and leave for work.

Liz waited for him to leave and then she came out of the bedroom and had some breakfast and quickly went to work. Liz worked for a laundry company but hated the work. Cleaning other people's dirty underwear was not her idea of a good time. But she dreamed of the cash that her father may have in the bank from his days as rock star. That could help her out amazingly. The only problem was that she couldn't walk away from Eli; she just didn't have the courage. And it wasn't that she was afraid he would beat her up—that had happened a few times in the past. The problem was that he had convinced her that she needed him for protection. Back in the days when Liz was actively singing, Eli fancied himself as a roadie, bodyguard, head of security, whatever his fantasy was that day. And at first, Liz liked the attention that he poured on her. But it was all part of the grooming process that he was slowly but surely infusing into her life. Liz wouldn't say that she was head over heels for him, but part of her mind wouldn't let her walk away from him.

A week went by, and Liz was going to the hospital to get her DNA results. Liz walked out of her house thinking Eli had already left. She closed the door, Eli was there standing in front of her and with a swoosh he swung two dozen roses from behind his back to under her chin.

"Let's try to work things out, sweetie," he said.

Wow, he still can't say those two words. It is almost like it is a foreign language to him, she surmised.

Liz backed up to get the two dozen roses out of her face.

"Eli, what are you doing?"

"I am trying to give my girlfriend a couple dozen roses. Why are you being so weird?" he said using the time-honored technique of turning the blame around on the victim.

"Well, Eli, you don't just shove the flowers in my face."

Damn, he thought, *I am on my best behavior right now.*

But Eli Anselmi had a hard time with good behavior. He turned around and threw the roses as far as he could.

"Why are you always so pissed off?" Liz asked.

"I just did something amazingly thoughtful for you. And you are the one who is pissed off."

"Why don't we just take some more time off?" she said.

"But, Liz, I am here to support you like I was doing the day that you passed out."

She looked at the half circle of bruises which were just visible under the sunglasses. That made her shake her head, but also feel incredibly guilty.

"All right, you can come to the lab with me," she said.

"Yeah, you need help to deal with this, sweetie," Eli said as he produced his best fake smile.

"Okay, but I don't want you to say anything at the lab."

"Well, just be careful not look at any blood."

Eli slid his hand into her hand and interlaced their fingers.

They walked into the lab, and the head phlebotomist clandestinely rolled her eyes as she saw the couple approaching.

I can't believe she got back together with that guy, she thought.

"Hello, Ms. Gillette, how are you feeling?"

"I'm fine, but we are here to get my DNA results."

The guy with the sunglasses on didn't utter a word. The lab worker glanced at him and gave a slight smile and a head nod.

"Okay, I will print the results out for you."

Eli never released her hand as the lab technician talked to her. She walked over to the printer and picked up the papers and handed them to Liz. Eli glanced at the results.

"Well, I can't understand this, there are just a bunch of numbers on this."

"Yes that is how DNA tests look," the tech said. "You will need to talk to your doctor and that person will interpret the results for you."

"Shit," Eli muttered out.

"Oh… Okay," Liz said.

Then the two of them walked back out the door of the lab.

"I didn't know this was going to be this difficult," she sighed.

"Yeah and once we get yours figured out, how are we going to get Roscoe's?"

"You are right. He would have to give his permission."

"Like I said, damned if you don't, damned if you do."

CHAPTER 13

1970

In the operating room, the trepanation tool had a high-pitched whine as the neurosurgeon cut her skull. The odor of the burning bone was heavy in the air. And could be smelled through the masks. He cut half of her skull off and the lifted the piece of bone away and put it in a saline bath. The piece would be replaced at a later time once the swelling was under control. As the surgeon watched the exposed dura matter of Kandace's brain, he could see it expanding and knew it was only a matter of time; even if the swelling didn't kill her, an infection could easily set in and finish her off. The doctor ordered a massive dose of antibiotics to control infections, but all of it was for naught. Twelve hours after the accident, the neurosurgeon was sitting in the doctors' lounge when he heard the overhead page.

"Code blue, ICU."

"Code blue, ICU."

"Code blue, ICU."

The cardiac arrest team ran to the unit with a Lifepack 5. They stripped the hospital gown off her and noticed a slight blueish hue to her face. Hence, the name. Then the leader of the team put the paddles on the center of her sternum and on her lower left ribcage.

"Charging to two hundred!" the leader said.

The Lifepack whined with a very high pitch and that was followed by more orders.

"Clear!"

The entire team stopped CPR, and everything else they were doing and returned with a response, "Clear."

Then he depressed the buttons and an audible noise of a body being lifted up and dropping back down could be heard. He looked over at the monitor on the Lifepack, and the green horizontal line midway up the screen showed that the effort was far from over.

"Resume CPR," he said.

"Charging to three hundred," he said.

The high-pitched whine started all over again and that was followed by all the other steps in the sequence, which was then finished off by a depressed statement: "Flat line."

There was one more step as practiced a million times by the team.

"Charge to 360."

When that failed, the doctor leading the team said, "I am calling this," and he looked at his watch.

"Time of death, 3:10 p.m. or 7:00 a.m."

A nurse that was keeping records wrote the time in the appropriate box. The team left very dejected. They hated failing and each one of them racked their brains to try and figure out if they could have done anything better to save this girl.

The next day, everyone involved in Kandace's care met for a discussion about what they could have done better. But the fact was that some people just can't be saved, and when the team responded and saw an exposed brain, they were shocked, and many of them thought: *This is just a practice run.*

However, there were no tears. The majority of people what work in medicine are used to seeing death in its most gruesome forms.

"Code blue."

Bill Jenkins immediately tensed in his waiting room chair. He knew the news even before being told. Five minutes later, the hospital chaplain walked into the waiting room, and Bill went from rage to a blubbering man whose sobs shook his entire body with great heaves. As the chaplain walked up to him, Bill let out a guttural scream, "Nooo Don't take my girl!"

The other people in the waiting room were startled when Bill Jenkins screamed.

"Sir, she is with the Lord."

"Well, I didn't say the Lord could have her! You think it makes everything okay to say she is with the Lord. Well, it doesn't."

"I am so sorry for your loss."

Bill and Ethel cried uncontrollably for an hour. Then Bill suddenly stood up. "I want to see my daughter!"

"Sir, you don't want to see her like this."

"No, Bill," Ethel said as she grabbed his arm.

He shook himself free of the grasp and stormed into the ICU.

"Where is Kandace?"

"Sir, this is not a good time."

He nearly bowled her over, saying, "Well, when will it be a good time?"

When Bill got into Kandace's room, she was covered with a sheet. He pulled the sheet back and that's when he saw the trepanation and the exposed gray matter. For a moment, Bill Jenkins couldn't catch his breath. And as the sight that was lying before him began to sink in, the man that was standing as frozen as a statue began to heave. He turned and ran out of the room and made it to the hallway before his stomach emptied. He was running like a blind man from a demon that he had just seen. Unfortunately, he didn't see the pile of vomit that he had just produced, and when his foot hit it, the rug was pulled out from under him. His back hit square on the floor, and it was at least a minute before he came around.

Jamie's situation was not that much better. A femur fracture and many other injuries including second-degree burns on the non-fractured leg. Thirty percent of her legs and lower abdomen had second-degree burns. Also a large amount of blood loss had taken her close to the void. Only the skill of the emergency responders managed to snatch her back from of the void.

At one point, she saw a brilliant white light that scared her. She wanted to run from the light and go back to her warm bed. She also made it to the ICU an hour behind Kandace. Because of the blood loss, her heart stopped twice and the code team had much better luck with Jamie. They brought her back to the land of the living and switched off the white light. Then she was rolled into the ICU. When the cleaning crew started working on that OR suite, they had a big job to do. There was blood everywhere, the bed was saturated, the floor was covered. And even the big light above the bed needed to be wiped down.

Jamie was given a thirty percent chance of survival. But then the surgeons often shot low, then if they survived, it was a miracle, and if they didn't, it would probably come out around the percentage that was given. And who really had an idea of what thirty percent was? Was it an element of time or an quantity of injuries or maybe it was a quotient of luck. But no one in medicine would attempt to calculate luck even if that was possible. In other words, if she made it twenty-four hours, would her chance of survival go up to fifty percent? Or if she had three major organs affected by trauma, then her chance of survival went down to twenty percent. The surgeons must have a formula for coming up with this chance of survival. And basically, the unknowing public celebrated if it was over fifty percent and got depressed if it was under.

One of the bad things for Jamie was she had so many different types of injuries that it was difficult to know where to start. But of course, the hypovolemic shock took the lead because it would kill her the quickest. At the same time, the major fractures had to be dealt with because they were causing the shock. And that left the burns to bring up the end. But the surgeons were good and experienced, and they knew how to work on patients with multiple injuries and how to respect the other person's space to the benefit of the patient. There were no arguments, but there were disagreements, and each person put their opinion forward, and the one with the most convincing point usually got their way.

The accident and the multiple surgeries were just the beginning for Jamie. After a week of constant surgeries, she started six months in a half-body cast which allowed her femurs to heal. She also needed a lot of therapy because of the loss of her best friend and the difficulties of being trapped in a plaster prison. She had to be catheterized, and the daily bedpan ritual had to be the most embarrassing things anyone could go through. After six months of incarceration, Jamie was cut out of the cast, and the room filled with a dust cloud and the smell of plaster dust. That wasn't her favorite experience, but it was the road to freedom.

When the cast was gone she realized that freedom was a long way off. Her muscles had atrophied, and she could barely move them. The physical therapy started immediately, and her very weak body had a hard time recovering. But the daily workouts began to get easier as her muscles recovered their strength. She went from bedridden to cruising around the hospital in a wheelchair. Luckily for Jamie, she had kept the strength in her arms by lifting weights which were ever increasingly heavier.

Unfortunately, her legs looked like sticks with thin ropes hanging from them. At first, she could only exercise for about an hour, but over the first month, she was up to five hours. Jamie was so eager to walk again that, some days, she continued the exercises after the physical therapist left. Her legs had two long scars on them. Although the fracture on her left leg was just a little worse than a hairline fracture, the right side had a compound fracture that kept getting infected, and the cast had to be removed a few times so the wound could be debrided. Then a new cast would be put on, and the wait would continue. The next day, the physical therapist would be back for another round. Jamie would drag herself out of her bed and into the wheelchair and go for long cruises around the hospital. She met a lot of people in a similar situation as herself, and they formed a club called the Chair Warriors. People would come and go from the hospital as they healed and new people got injured.

Occasionally, a person would die, but that was usually early in their stay before Jamie got to know them. But a few of her friends expired from blood clots or infections. That brought her down in a new low and eventually she stopped meeting new people because the pain of losing people was too harsh. Eventually, she walked out of the hospital under her own power. That was a day of celebration and her parents took her home for the rest of her recovery.

CHAPTER 14

2005

Liz went to see John at the hospital to ask him some questions about Roscoe.

"How are you doing, Liz?" John asked.

"I am doing okay, but I can't figure out these DNA results, and I was hoping you could help me out."

"Sure," he said as he glanced at the paper she had brought with her. "Well, according to the results on this paper, it basically states that Roscoe Gillette is, in fact, your father.

"Oh my goodness," she said as she felt her eyes tearing up.

"How you doing with all the changes in your life?"

"It has rocked my world," Liz said.

"I'm sure it has. What else can I help you with?"

"I'm not sure how to go about this with my dad."

"Have you raised any children, Liz?"

"No. No children," she said with a despondent tone in her voice.

"It's okay. Lots of people go through life just fine with no children. But no worries. You are a very smart lady, and I am sure you could pick this up easily.

"Well… Actually, John, I had a child, but I lost her of my stupidity," Liz said.

"Oh I am sorry, Liz, but you are not a stupid person."

"How is that? It is easier to take care of an adult than a child, isn't it?"

"Well, actually your dad has the mind of a three-year-old, maybe a five-year-old on a good day."

"Well, I don't know what to say. I don't have any experience with kids. Will I have to change diapers?"

"Well, actually, that's a good question, Roscoe does wear diapers, and yes, you will have to change them or hire someone to do that for you."

"But I don't have the money to hire people."

"Yes, and that is the other big issue, your dad's money. You will have to go through some major twists and turns to access that money."

"And why is that? If the DNA results prove that I am his daughter, it should be the way that I can take care of him."

"Yes, and eventually, you will be able to get that, but to start with, you should probably use his Medicare or Medicaid and the hospital is looking into that. So if it works out, things might come together just fine."

"I hope so because Eli is pretty upset by all of this."

"Yes… And I am glad that you came this time by yourself because I wanted to talk to you alone."

Liz started to feel the heat building upon her face as a full-on blush hit its max.

"Yeah," she said nodding her head. Her eyes were cast down at the floor.

"Are things okay at home?"

"Ah yeah, I guess."

"Well, I don't want to release Roscoe into a violent situation, and I think you should remove yourself from any situation that would harm you."

Liz began crying and shaking her head.

"If I leave Eli, he will kill me!"

"Has he threatened you?"

"Not really. Well, maybe… Yeah, but it was a long time ago."

"Why on earth would you stay with this guy?"

"I am afraid of being alone."

"You are a very attractive woman. There are a lot of men that would be very good to you."

"I just have a way of finding the creeps."

"Only if you want to find the creeps. If you insist on finding a good man, you will."

Another long episode of the waterworks ensued.

"Okay, let's change the subject," John said as he handed her a box of facial tissues.

"Okay," she choked out.

"We started this conversation about your father. So the hospital is going to try to get money from you to pay for your father's care, since you are the only living relative, and he has racked up a pretty substantial bill."

"But I don't have the money for that, and Eli will be so pissed."

"Well, two things," he said, holding up two fingers. "The hospital may be able to access money from Medicare. And then they will go after the money he has stashed away from his days in music."

"You mean the money in the banks?"

"Yes, ma'am."

"That's why Eli is going to be so pissed."

"Again, Ms. Gillette, if you give your life away. There are plenty of people who are willing take it."

"I know," she said with a frown on her face.

"If you want to take care of your dad, it won't be an easy road. You will have to watch him, pretty much 24-7. Because if you leave an Alzheimer's patient alone, they will be confused, and they may just wander away. There are memory care facilities, and they keep their patients in total lockdown for that exact reason. And they are fairly expensive. Your father's savings would probably take care of that for a while. It also won't be easy to get the money out of the banks because if it were easy, the bad guys would be going to the banks and saying all kinds of things to get money from people they don't even know. But you have done the most important part, and that is you have proved that you are his daughter with the DNA test.

"You know the other thing that bothers me is that he thinks that I am either my mom or his mother."

"I can almost guarantee you that he thinks that you are your mother because you said that you and your mother have one and the same looks. But they weren't married, were they?" John said.

"No. The best I can figure it out, it was a one-night stand."

"When did your mom pass away?"

"Ten years ago."

"From what?"

"Ovarian cancer."

"Well, it is hard to figure out what the mind retains and what it forgets, but he has your mom firmly affixed in his memory."

"It was probably his first love."

"Yes, so that is often something that is burned into our memories—our first love."

"And since I look so much like my mother, he thinks I am her."

"That's very possible. It is hard to know what is going on inside his mind."

"Well, when will he be released from the hospital."

"He could be released in a couple days. It kind of depends on whether you are willing to take him in."

"And if I can't take him in, where will he go?"

"Well, I will have to get to work and find a memory care facility or a senior residence that could handle this kind of a patient."

Liz let out a long sigh and shook her head as she thought all the things they had talked about.

"I'll be in touch with you," she said.

"Okay, I'll be here. And, Liz? Take care of yourself. And you know what I mean by that."

Liz just nodded in silence.

Liz went back to her house and Eli was home.

"Eli, we need to talk."

"Yeah, we do. Where have you been?" he said.

"I was just at the hospital talking to John about Roscoe."

"And you didn't invite me? Are you hiding something from me?"

"I have never hidden anything from you!"

"Good. Let's keep it that way. So what did you find out?"

"I had John interpret the DNA results for me."

"Yeah, so?"

"Eli… Roscoe is my father."

"Yes," Eli said with both his fists clenched.

"I think I am going to have to take care of him."

"And what does that mean?"

"Well, one thing that that means is he is going to have to move in here."

"What! Where the hell is he going to sleep?"

"We will clean out the spare bedroom, and he will sleep in there."

"Where am I going to hang my punching bag?"

"I have never liked that thing in the first place, and you can hang it in the garage."

"And who's going to take care of the old man? Liz, you are not a nurse, and I sure as hell am not a nurse!"

"He won't need a nurse once he is released from the hospital. But I will need your help."

"And what do you want me to do?"

"All you have to do is watch the guy so he doesn't wander away."

"Liz, you are asking too much of me. What if the guy croaks?"

"We are all going to die someday."

Eli stopped and thought for a moment. Then a smile came to his face.

"Oh, I see where you are going with this," he said.

"No, I'm not! Look, Eli, Roscoe is my only living relative!" she said.

"And will you be able to get his fortune?"

"Well, no, not exactly."

"Not exactly! If you screw this up, I am going to kick your ass."

"It's not about money, it's about family!" she shouted.

"Well, guess what, we can't live on love alone!"

"Look, John said the hospital will have to get paid first because Roscoe has run up a good bill."

"How much does he have?"

"It's going to take some time to figure that out."

"Well, we don't make enough to take care of a sick old man. So you better work extra hard to figure that out."

"I am trying, Eli, but look, if this is too stressful, you can move out and live the life you want. I have to do this."

"The old man dumped you before you were born, why are you working so hard to save the guy?"

"Because family comes first and I can forgive. Apparently, that's a word you have never heard."

Two days later, Liz went to the hospital, and with John's help, Roscoe was discharged from the hospital.

"Roscoe, this is your daughter, Liz. She is going to take you home."

Roscoe had a very confused look on his face. He shook his head and then held out both of his hands, "Mom," he said.

Liz looked to John for support, and John tilted his head toward Roscoe.

Liz cleared her throat and walked over to Roscoe. "Roscoe, my name is Liz," she said as she felt the tears welling up in her eyes.

"Roscoe, Liz is neither your mother or anybody else's mother. But she is your child."

They stood and watched the confused look develop on Roscoe's face. And then he shook his head and looked from one to the other.

"Mom?"

John jumped in again. He pointed to Liz and said, "Liz."

Roscoe shook his head again.

"Mom?" he said.

"Well, it's going to take time to talk him out of that and maybe he will never be able to make that connection and maybe he will never be able to shake that thought."

"Roscoe, do you want to come with me?" Liz said as she held her hand out.

Roscoe had a big smile on his face, and he reached out and took her hand. Then Liz and Roscoe got into the car, and John walked around to the driver's side window.

"I'm sure you will do fine, Liz. Remember, you want to do this from your heart."

Liz swallowed deeply and had a sheepish smile on her face.

"Don't worry, Liz. You will fit right into this role. Just give it a week, and you will see. Things will start to come together."

"Thanks for your help," She said.

They drove away from the hospital, and Roscoe was very content. He felt like he was in exactly the right place. Even though he wasn't exactly sure were that place was.

CHAPTER 15

2005

As a bouncer in a couple of bars, Eli had most of his days off because he worked nights. The spare bedroom in the house that he and Liz shared had a punching bag hanging from a sturdy rafter and actually had several different bags in the spare room.

Right now, Eli was pounding hard on the fifty-pound body bag, and he was trying to get his anger out on the bag. When he was finished, he pulled the earbuds out of his ears.

How could she move her father into this room? This is my gym! he thought.

A few more shots at the body bag, then he pulled the boxing gloves off and threw them in the corner them into the corner of the room. As he headed for the shower, he had to cut through the living room. As he turned the corner into the living room, he was face-to-face with Roscoe and Liz. Everyone was a little startled, and when they got over the shock, Liz stepped back a couple steps because she could read Eli's face. He burst into a tirade.

"Liz, do you know what happens when you sneak up on someone in their house?"

"My house, Eli."

"We have shared this house since I saved your ass from that fool you used to date."

"Yes, but my mom bought this house and paid it off through her hard work, and then she died and I inherited it."

"So?"

"My house."

"So?"

"If I want to move my dad into this house, that's what will happen."

"Thanks for thinking of the man that has protected you through thick and thin."

"I am thinking of everyone under this roof, but I couldn't care less about a punching bag. I want it down by the time the sun goes down!"

"Shit, Liz, this is so unfair!"

"Why don't you whine like a five-year-old?"

Roscoe watched with a slight smile on his face unsure about what was going on. Eli slammed the front door as he walked out. A picture of Becky fell off the wall, and hit the floor. Liz walked over to Roscoe who had a look of fear on his face. She held her arms open, and they embraced.

"Why is he so mad?" Roscoe asked.

"That's just the way he is," Liz replied.

"I do something wrong?" Roscoe asked.

"No, you did nothing wrong. This is going to be your new bedroom."

Roscoe pointed to his chest. "Mine?"

"Yes."

Liz knew that Eli would not come back because he thought if he did not take the punching bag down, it would just hang there. She then looked at the bag and saw the heavy webbing straps sewed into the top of the bag. She went into the kitchen and took a serrated knife out of a kitchen drawer. Then she got a three-step ladder out of the garage and dragged it into the spare bedroom.

Over the next few hours, she sawed away at the straps on the top of the bag. As the last strap was cut almost through, she heard a ripping sound of fabric tearing. The fifty-pound bag dropped to the floor and fell over, knocking the ladder over and tossing Liz to the floor. She hit her head on the wall and was rendered unconscious. Roscoe was confused and walked over to the unconscious woman. He gazed at Liz and tapped her shoulder.

"Mom?"

Roscoe bent down and put his hand on her shoulder and shook as hard as he could. Liz was out like a light and was completely unresponsive. Roscoe looked around the room and didn't know what to do with this situation. He walked out of the spare bedroom trying to figure out what to do next. He looked around the living room not recognizing anything. Then he went around the room trying all the doors. The first two were a closet and the bathroom. All Roscoe could do is shake his head and the fear of the unknown started to build up until he was hyperventilating. In about ten minutes, his hands began to tingle. He started to panic, and then he found the last door in the room and quickly swung it open and was teetering in front of a black void.

1970

After a six-month stay in the hospital, Jamie was released, and her father drove her home. She had talked to a psychologist though out her recovery in the hospital and that had helped her deal with the loss of her best friend Kandace.

She had missed the funeral, and so she had asked her father to take her to the cemetery first so she could give her respects. When they had arrived at the cemetery and parked the car, they took the long walk through all the gravestones with names and dates carved into them. Finally, they arrived at a small stone with Kandace's name on it. Jamie stood there in the still fresh dirt and stared. She had forearm crutches to assist with walking, and she had gotten really good with them and had no problem weaving through the graves. As she stood in front of Kandace's grave, there were some questions heavy on her mind.

"So why do people do this?"

"Do what?"

"Why do people dig deep holes, lower a concrete vault down into it, and then a heavy wooden casket goes into that, then a concrete top is lowered onto the vault and then a bunch of dirt is dumped into the hole? Oh, and I forgot, there is a dead body in the center of all this."

"Well, I guess, it is a tribute to the person."

"I know, but why save the body? Do people think that the corpse can be brought back to life?"

"Well, I am not sure I have an answer to that. This is just a tradition that people have done for centuries."

"Is it a religious ritual?"

"Well, yes and no."

"But isn't it just a waste of land?"

"It depends on your perspective."

"If I would have died in that crash is, this where I would be right now?"

"Probably."

"So you aren't sure of what you would have done with me."

"Your mom and I were forced to discuss this after the accident, but because of your will to live, we didn't have to make that difficult final decision."

"Have you ever considered cremation?"

"Well, some religions don't like cremation because it symbolizes hell."

"But I thought the soul escaped the body once death occurred."

"Well, I am glad you are asking these questions, but I am not sure I am equipped to answer all of them. Why don't you talk to the minister at the church?"

"Because you are my father, of that I am sure, but I don't know the minster that well. And I trust you, Dad. And you and Mom pulled me back from the brink of death."

"Wow, thank you, sweetie."

"No. Thank you, dad."

"You are welcome. A part of my life would have ended if I had lost you."

They stayed at the gravestone, and Jamie was quiet for the rest of the time and just kept in her own mind as she stared at a beautiful sunset in progress. She pointed at the sunset.

"I think that is Kandace saying goodbye to me," Jamie said.

"Well, we can stay as long as we need to sweetie."

"No, I think I am ready to go home."

She used her crutches to get herself back to the car. Once they were in the car, her dad looked at her to make sure she was ready.

"Thanks, Dad, for doing this for me."

"You're welcome."

They drove back to their house. When Jamie got to her house, she got on the phone and called the other girls. She was on the phone for hours. And then when she finally fell asleep, it was a fitful sleep.

1970

Roscoe had long since vanished on another tour to many cities around the country. It had been six months since the accident. He was meeting many girls in all parts of the country and was the father to an unknown amount of children. For some reason, his first love, Becky, stayed enmeshed in his memory despite how many women he slept with. Many girls followed 'til it got to a point where he couldn't even remember their names and relied on terms of endearment like *baby* and *sweetie* to get by the embarrassment.

Roscoe started drinking pretty heavy, and eventually, at every gig, audience members would buy the band a round of drinks. And it never ended. At one gig, he pushed the piano bench back, grabbed the mic, and started dancing around the stage. When he staggered near the front of the stage, the bright lights disoriented him until the next step was into nothingness. Luckily, he landed on two audience members, who probably saved his life.

Nate pushed his way through the crowd and picked him up. But Roscoe was a violent drunk and as soon as he was upright, he took a couple swings at Nate. Then he lost his balance and fell again. The concert had to be cancelled halfway through, and the Backdoor Brothers lost another venue.

The heavy alcohol use at such a young age, before his mind had fully developed, set him on a course that would end with Alzheimer's. The only amazing thing was that he had any money in the bank because alcoholics were notorious for giving away all their money or losing all their money. Somehow, Roscoe had started so many bank accounts around the country, and he had forgotten many of them.

2005

The hospital was actively checking all the banks in the areas that the band played. They found money in many banks and then they proceeded with legal actions to get the money that they had spent to take care of him.

* * *

Roscoe was standing in front of the black void, swaying back and forth. His pants were tucked up halfway between his hips and his ribcage. He wasn't sure what to do at this point, but there was a bit of fear in him as he stared into blackness. He stood and shook his head as he tried to figure his dilemma out.

The only thing that came out of his mouth was "Mom?"

CHAPTER 16

2005

Eli walked into the local bar in an extremely foul mood. It was early and the only one in the bar was the regulars. Eight patrons that started every day in the bar and ended every day in the bar. This was breakfast, lunch, and dinner for them. He walked up to the bar and pounded his fist down and said, "Bar keep!"

"What do ya need?" the bartender asked.

"Whiskey."

"You want Rot Gut or do you have a brand in mind?"

"Whatever the cheapest is."

The bartender set the shot glass down with a loud click, causing some of the whiskey to spill out. When the whiskey hit the bar, Eli could smell the aroma of fresh whiskey, which was better than whiskey breath coming from the mouths of the eight alcoholics. Most of the drinkers had only a couple of teeth left in their mouth.

Then suddenly, a woman who was at the bar and was already drunk at 1:00 p.m. leaned back and fell off the bar stool. She hit her head on the concrete floor. Nobody in the bar even noticed that the woman had taken a dive. Eli who was the one at the bar who was not yet drunk looked over when he heard her skull crack like an egg. He saw the crimson blood forming under her hair.

"Hey, bartender, that chick isn't moving. You might want to call an ambulance."

"No, she does that all the time."

"Well, whatever you say, but I doubt that she does this that often."

Eli lifted the glass to his lips and threw the booze back into his throat. He felt the burn of the alcohol, and swallowed it down.

"Look, dude, I work at a couple bars, and if I saw this, I would be on the phone calling someone."

The bartender set a dial phone on the bar in front of Eli.

"Knock yourself out," the bartender said.

Eli picked up the phone and tried to remember how these worked. He lifted the receiver and spun the dial to call 911. When he was done, he slid the phone back. Still no one in the bar even commented on what was going on. The ambulance arrived, and the EMTs rolled a stretcher into the bar and lifted the unconscious woman up to it. Then they placed two 4x4s onto the laceration onto the parietal region of her skull and wrapped her head with roller Kling. They tried some ammonia salts under her nose to no avail. She was definitely out cold. Then they rolled her out of the bar.

"See ya next time, Pete," the EMT said.

"Hmm," the bar tender responded.

1970

Roscoe finished a concert in Houston, and he was walking backstage where he met a twenty-something woman. And this woman had class. After being around a bunch of squealing teenagers that frequented the Backdoor Brothers shows, he was intrigued. She spoke with a husky voice and that gave her an exotic allure. He thought he heard a slight foreign accent. They had a few drinks, and one thing lead to another, and within a few hours, they were in bed together.

As was traditional, Roscoe left in the morning to rejoin the tour. And as was also like always, he was late, and the tour was waiting for him. Within two weeks, Roscoe started to feel some pain and itching in his urethra. When he urinated, the pain intensified. He was taking his underwear off one night, and his penis was stuck to the fabric. When he looked at his urethra, he saw a thick yellowish drop of discharge ready to exit his urethra. Then he saw the yellow stain in his underwear. He found Nate in his hotel room.

"Nate, I need help."

"You need more than help."

"I got shit dripping out of my cock!"

"Literally, shit?"

"You know, I have some yellowish creamy stuff dripping out of my thing, and it burns like hell every time I pee! And it is freaking me out."

"Your 'thing'?"

"You know where I pee from."

Nate knew Roscoe was immature, but this was a whole new challenge.

"Have you been sexually active recently?"

"Sexually active? Do you mean have I had sex? Yeah, like every night!"

"Do you wear condoms?"

"Nobody told me I was supposed to!"

"Nobody told you to breathe, how did you figure that one out?"

"Shut up!"

"How much discomfort are you in?"

"How much? A lot!"

"On a scale of 1 to 10, how much pain are you feeling?"

"Well, it is my thing, you know, so any pain scares me!"

"Well, why don't we call it your penis, and let's go back to the 1 to 10 scale."

"I don't know. I guess an eight."

"Okay, well, I will find a clinic in the next town, and we will get you checked out."

"Next town?"

"Well, we will never get into any place today. And I am going to buy you a box of condoms, since you can't keep it in your pants. Every time you want to have sex, put a condom on. Every time."

When they arrived, in the next town, Nate drove Roscoe to the clinic. Roscoe was sweating when they went into a room.

"Dude, you aren't going to stay here, are you?"

Nate laughed and walked out of the room. The doctor walked in with ten other people. This was a teaching hospital. Roscoe was beside himself with anxiety as he scanned the room of people.

"Look, this is not a time for my fan club," Roscoe replied.

"These people need to see everything to learn, and they are all professionals."

"I thought you would just give me something for this problem."

"Well, you certainly have the right to leave if you want to, but we can't treat you unless we examine you."

All the people put gloves on and looked at him a little closer then he would have liked. A few of them moved his penis around for a better look. The sweat was literally dripping off his face. Then the doctor took a long cotton swab and walked up to Roscoe and slid the swap into his urethra. Roscoe was literally squirming with the pain and discomfort. He was hyperventilating and felt like he was going to faint. Finally, he removed the swap and put it in a tube to seal it.

"Are you going to able to fix this today?" Roscoe asked.

The doctor chuckled.

"I don't even know what it is yet, so no."

"Well, haven't you seen this before?"

"Lots of things present like this, so when we get the results back from the lab, we will know how to treat it."

"But I am on tour with the Backdoor Brothers, and we are leaving tomorrow."

"The who?"

"Not The Who! the Backdoor Brothers!" he said to a chorus of chuckles from the crowd.

"I'm sorry, young man. I'm not sure what you are talking about."

"I am the lead singer with a band!"

"Okay, well, what I can do is give you an antibiotic that will knock out some diseases. We will try tetracycline first, and if that doesn't work, fill this prescription for Amoxicillin, and maybe we will get this taken care of.

"Oh, and Mr. Gillette, here is a box of condoms. Don't have unprotected sex with anyone until this clears up, and after that, use these condoms to protect yourself."

"You sound just like my manager, no fun."

"Well, young man, one day you may confront something that will take all the fun out of your life."

He shook hands with Roscoe and then immediately got some alcohol gel and washed his hands with it. When Roscoe got back to the band, no one would get near him.

2005

As Roscoe stood there, peering into the darkness, a hand touched his back. A momentary pause as Roscoe realized that there was someone else in the room. Then another hand grabbed his upper arm. He put his hands against the door frame to stabilize himself.

"Dad?" a groggy voice said.

Then Liz dropped to her knees holding on to Roscoe. She was still very dizzy after her fall. Roscoe turned around and looked at the woman.

"Mom?"

"No, no, Roscoe. I'm not your mother!"

"What?"

"Roscoe, I need help."

"Help?"

"Yes, can you call 911?"

"Call?"

"Yes, pick up the phone and dial 911."

"Phone?"

She tried to stand and the room spinning dizziness kicked in and she covered her eyes to get control of the vertigo. She dropped to the floor to get control of herself.

"Hand me the phone."

"I don't know."

She grabbed the counter and tried to pull herself up to get the phone. She felt around on the counter top until she touched the phone. Because of the dizziness she couldn't open her eyes. Then she felt the key pad to find the numbers. The first five attempts got nothing. Then she succeeded.

"911, where's your emergency?"
"I'm at my house."
"What's your address, ma'am?"
"312 Smith Street."
"What's your emergency?"
"I got very dizzy and I hit my head on the wall."
"Did you lose consciousness?"
"I think I did."
"Okay, ma'am. The ambulance is on the way."
"Thank you."

Eli had left the door open when he left, and the medics knocked and then walked in. Liz still had her eyes covered and could not see the people who had entered. Liz explained what was going on with Roscoe and then asked if he could go to the hospital with her. They said yes, and then they started an intravenous line and then packed her into the ambulance and went to the hospital. Roscoe was confused about what was going on but just stayed with Liz, not wanting to leave her.

CHAPTER 17

1980

Becky woke up with a terrible headache. She never had migraines, so this episode took her by surprise. Now when she stood up quickly from a sitting position, the pain would shoot from the base of her skull to the top. She was also very nauseated, and once she got control of her body enough to walk across the room, she would be running to the bathroom to vomit.

Liz did her best to take care of her mom. It was difficult at best, mostly because of the personality changes. Her mom went from kind to extremely pissed off in less than a minute. Liz left her mom at least five times because of her blow-ups but always gave in and returned to help her out. In Liz's eyes, family came first.

Since the buildup was slow, Becky never really sought out medical care. She just thought it was part of getting older. After seventeen years of getting worse and worse, she became virtually unable to function. This made Liz grow up in a hurry, long before her time to become an adult.

But this also made Liz lean on men that were less than good for her. She liked the tough guys, but the tough guys she chose were tough guys because they took control of everything, whether they understood it or not. They were woefully short on the kindness spectrum, not to mention the intelligence spectrum. But Liz had felt alone with her mom for the majority of her young life.

Liz was driving since she was fifteen. High school was in the trash can because she was so busy taking her mom to doctor's appointments and all the myriad of other medical tests and visits. There were no more general practitioners; the medical field had a way of having every little thing a specialty. She flunked out of high school despite the teachers and administrators being very sympathetic.

Becky had a seizure at least once a month. Whenever she stood up, she had a headache. Then she started having difficulty speaking, and her personality went south in a hurry, especially to the one person who was closest to her. That was Liz. Liz felt she could never do anything right for her mother. Her mother would blow up at the least provocation. Maybe that's why Liz was so used to her boyfriend blowing up at her, and maybe that's why she would not walk away from them. Then after ten years of taking care of her mother, the brain tumor took her away from Liz. Liz immediately felt alone and was actually angry that her mother would leave her.

Liz started a revolving door of boyfriends because she was searching for someone to take the place of her mom. To say she was lonely was an understatement, and the boyfriends didn't do that much to dissuade that.

2005

Liz and Roscoe were at the house. Eli was still a no-show. Liz didn't know where he was, but figured he was still pissed that his punching bag was now laying in a corner of the spare bedroom. Liz got Roscoe to come into the kitchen and got him to sit down at the kitchen table.

"Now, Roscoe, you see that door over there?" she said as she pointed to the door that opened to the basement stairs. Roscoe looked then nodded his head.

"You don't ever open that door again," she said.

Roscoe just nodded his head, and she wondered what was going on in that head of his. She heated up some soup on the stove and looked over her shoulder at Roscoe. She suddenly realized that this was another really dangerous item for him.

"Roscoe," she said.

He turned and then she said, "Don't ever go near this stove. This is very dangerous."

As she looked at him, he nodded, but she saw the vacant look his eyes. There was nothing behind those eyes.

"Okay, Mom."

She dropped her head and smiled, but she wanted to scream.

What does he mean by this repetitive title of Mom?

She was sure that she would never figure this out. Had he regressed to his childhood? No one would ever know. There was no way she would ever crack this nut. What was locked in his skull was forever lost. But finally she had the child she could never have naturally. She laid out some place mats. These were her favorite place mats because they looked like the keys of a piano, and she had always had a dream of playing the piano.

Roscoe came to life when he saw the ivories laid out in front of him. His eyes moved back and forth. His arthritic hands suddenly loosened up and started flowing over the keys. Liz had a radio playing, and there just happened to be a piano concerto playing. Roscoe's head tilted to one side as he heard the music and a huge smile came to his face. His fingers danced over the pseudo keys, and he heard the notes playing in his own mind or on the radio.

Liz's jaw dropped as she saw the transformation overcome him.

This is incredible! she thought.

She was ripped out of this mesmerized state by the sound of boiling soup splashing out of the pot and sizzling as it hit the stovetop. Liz flipped through the channels on the radio and found the oldies channel. This was definitely his world, and in addition to playing his fake piano, he started singing. Liz knew a lot of these songs and sang along. Eventually, they stopped the music, and Liz gave him some soup, but she could still hear his feet tapping on the floor.

Then in the middle of the fun time they were having, a song came on the radio. Liz froze as the words came out of the radio.

"Eli's comin', Eli's comin', you better hide your heart, your loving heart."

Roscoe sang along very mightily with a big grin on his face, and the piano accompaniment got him playing along on his place mat.

Then his fingers went in the bowl of soup causing the half full bowl of soup to spill all over the kitchen table. Roscoe let out a chuckle and then looked up at Liz, and she couldn't help but to laugh as well. Roscoe and Liz cleaned up the soup all over the kitchen table and on the floor. They finished their lunch, and Liz was finishing cleaning up the kitchen table. As she walked past Roscoe's chair, he patted her on her butt. Liz immediately swung around and faced off with him.

"Roscoe, look, I am your daughter. I don't know what kind of relationship you and my mom had, but I am not my mother. It is inappropriate to do things like that," she replied.

He could sense that she was angry but for the life of him he couldn't figure out why. It was like she was disciplining a child. Unfortunately, she was woefully inexperienced at raising children. She had tried to get pregnant many times, but it never happened. She went to the hospital and had many tests to figure this problem out. In the end the ob-gyn doctor seemed to conclude it was polycystic ovarian syndrome, and the book was closed. Liz had lost her mother and now she would never have children and because of that, she dropped into deep depression.

Dating the thugs of this world was another waste of time, but she decided that even though she got beat up a few times, it was better than being alone. She was desperate for companionship but kept ending up with guys that only wanted one thing and that was sex. This drove her deeper into depression, and her interest in everything waned. And then there was Roscoe, and suddenly, she came to life. She had purpose in her life as long as she had him to take care of.

Eli swung the door of the house open and walked in with a slight swagger. Roscoe was still singing "Eli's coming, hide your heart girl." Liz was mopping up the kitchen floor.

"What the hell happened here?" Eli said.

"I just spilled some soup."

"What is he saying?"

"I don't know what he is saying."

"Well, it sounds like he keeps saying my name."

"Maybe he said, hello."

"He has never said hello to me before."

"Eli," Liz said.

"There he goes again."

"That was me," Liz said.

"Well, what do you want?"

"Could you find another place to live?" Liz swallowed deeply to calm her nerves.

"What?"

"You heard me," Liz said with a small smile on her face.

"Are you kicking me outta here?"

"I'm asking you for a favor."

"Yeah, everything I have done for you, and you think that kicking me out of the place that I live is a favor?" he said with his voice ratcheting up several octaves.

Eli stormed into the spare bedroom, and then he saw his punching bag laying on the floor. He then walked over to the bag and saw the cut straps.

"Liz!"

At this point, she knew she was in trouble for removing the punching bag, and she would have to pay with pain. Suddenly, Eli was back in the kitchen, and in the next second, he had her in a headlock. Roscoe was watching everything.

"Ah, ah, ah," was all that Roscoe could get out.

"'Ah, ah, ah.' Shit, is that all you can say? Liz your new bodyguard is stuttering," Eli shouted.

"Leave him alone, Eli."

Suddenly, Eli was dancing around the kitchen like a boxer, circling Roscoe.

"Come on old man protect your little girl. You know the one you left without even a dollar to her name."

Roscoe brought his hands up in fists.

"Look at this, Liz. He's ready to fight," Eli chided. Then Eli dropped his fists and was moving his head back and forth in front of Roscoe.

"Come on give it your best shot! Protect your little girl! Oh, what am I saying? You better protect Mom!"

Roscoe started breathing heavily. Then one of his arthritic hands shot forward. Eli quickly reached up with his hand and caught Roscoe's fist in his open palm. Roscoe's face immediately showed pain.

"Eli, don't hurt his hands!" Liz shouted.

"These aren't hands. They are just stumps," he said, laughing.

Then Liz wrapped her arms around Eli's waist and tried to pull him away from Roscoe.

"Look at this. I am being attacked by two people."

Then with his free hand, he grabbed Liz by the hair, and she screamed.

"Eli, I will give you anything, just don't hurt Roscoe. Let go this hand," she pleaded.

"Wait a minute, what did you just say? You will give me anything? Okay." he released both of them. "I'll start making up a list."

Liz started to sob because she was worried about Roscoe not being able to play the piano.

CHAPTER 18

1971

"Mother!"

"What's wrong, Becky?"

"I think I am having a baby!"

"Don't be ridiculous. Why are you playing jokes on me?"

"It's not a joke."

"But, honey, you have to be pregnant for nine months before you have a baby."

"It's been at least nine months for me," she said as she put her hands on her distended abdomen.

"Becky, you are just a heavy girl."

"Mother, I'm pregnant."

"Well, Becky, you have to do something else to be pregnant."

"I know, Mother!"

"Are you having sex?"

"Had sex."

"Who did you have sex with?"

"The love of my life."

"Okay, now I know you are joking. You are not only sixteen, but also you won't know the love of your life for a long time," Becky's mother chuckled.

"Owww!"

"What is wrong?"

"What are those pains called when you are having a baby?"

"You are not having contractions."

"Well, what's causing this pain?"
"Do you have an upset stomach?"
"Mother, I am pregnant!"
"Why are you breathing so hard?"
"That's what you're supposed to do when you are having a baby."
"Hey, why are you peeing all over the new carpet for?"
"My water just broke!"
"What the hell?"
"Could you call me an ambulance?"
"Why don't I give you a ride to the hospital?"
"You are not an ambulance, you crazy old lady!"
"But, honey, we don't have the money for an ambulance."
"Well, I'll just have my baby right here!"
"What are you talking about? I'm sorry to tell you this, Becky, but you are fat!"
"I'm fat because I have to eat for two now."
"Stop being so dramatic."
"Owwww!" Becky said holding her abdomen.

Her mother started to think that there was something to this. She picked up the phone and called her pediatrician.

"Hello, Dr. Caskey?"
"How is Becky doing?"
"Well, that's why I am calling. She is complaining of severe belly pain."
"Belly, meaning abdominal pain?"
"Yes."
"Well, I could do a house call, but I am busy at the office until four o'clock, By the way, has she vomited?"
"No, but she peed all over the new carpet."
"What do you mean 'peed'?"
"You know, urinated. And not a little bit—it was like a gallon!"
"Is she pregnant?"
"Don't be silly, Doctor. She's sixteen."
"Ma'am, I hate to break the news to you, but sixteen-year-olds have babies. I think you should take her to the hospital, and I will meet you there in about an hour."

"Don't you think if she sits on the toilet, she will be fine in about an hour?"

"Ma'am, you can do whatever you want, and I won't know until I examine her, but it sounds like she is pregnant."

"Okay, Doctor. Well, I'm going to try the toilet and see if that works. If not, I'll bring her to the hospital."

"Whatever you think, ma'am."

She walked into the living room. "The doctor wants you to have a bowel movement."

"Owww! Mother, my guts feel like they are exploding!"

"Well, sit on the toilet and maybe you can get rid of this."

"Mother, you are crazy? People don't have babies in their bathrooms!"

"Well, if I take you to the hospital, they will charge me more money than I have. And you just peed all over my new carpet."

Becky crawled to the toilet and even managed to lift herself into a sitting position. She felt like she was going to pass out.

"Mother, I need to go to the hospital!"

"Becky, why do you think you are pregnant?"

"Mom, what are you thinking? My water broke. Pretty soon, a baby will drop into this toilet. Do you want your grandchild to be born in a toilet?"

1986

"Hi, Mom," Liz said.

"Hi, sweetie," Becky said with a puny tone.

"How are you?"

"I have a headache."

"You have had a headache every day for the last week."

"Really? Just a week?"

"Well, how long have you had a headache?"

"Forever."

"Right… You have had a headache every day of your life."

"I have felt pain in my head every day for a long time. Sometimes mild, sometimes intense."

"Well, why don't you see a doctor?"

"Doctors cost money."

"You've heard of Medicaid, haven't you?"

"I just want to sleep."

"Okay."

Liz made an appointment with a neurologist, and a month later, Becky and Liz were in a neurologist's office.

"Hello, ladies."

"Hello, Dr. Paddock."

"So what's going on today?"

Becky was sitting in the chair with her head in her hands.

"My mom has headaches all the time."

"Is that right, ma'am?" he said, trying to get her to speak.

"Yes, I have at least a small headache every day and often a major headache," she said.

The doctor noticed a speech impediment, and he knew that was a bad sign.

"Well, we will have to utilize a new technology, and it's called a CAT scan."

"Oh, great. Now medicine is being run by a bunch of cats."

"Yes, ma'am. That's an acronym for computed axial tomography."

"Great, the gibberish really helps too."

"My apologies, ma'am. It is an advanced x-ray of the brain. So we can see if there are any problems that we would have to address."

"But I don't have the money for the basic stuff, and it goes without saying that don't have the money for the advanced stuff."

"Okay, well let's go back to the more basic tests and then you can make decisions as we go if we have positive tests. Nurse, let's draw some blood, and I am going to order a CA 125," he said to the nurse.

"Okay, Doctor," the nurse said.

"Becky, the nurse is going to draw some blood, and we are going to do some tests that will give us a better idea if we need to order more tests."

"Thanks, Dr. Paddock."

"But you should think about what you want to do if the tests come back positive."

"If the tests come back positive, is that a death sentence?"

"Not necessarily, people survive cancer all the time. Do you have insurance, Becky?"

"Well, I have Medicaid, does that count?"

"Can she buy new insurance now, Doctor?" Liz chimed in.

"That's the problem with insurance companies, once you have a positive diagnosis, they won't even answer your phone calls."

"Well, Mother, I'm working, maybe I can get insurance for you."

"You heard what he said. If I am positive for cancer, they won't even talk to us."

* * *

The Backdoor Brothers were having a hard time on the music scene. A lot of the band had drifted away from the band mostly because of Roscoe's unpredictability. The band did well for the first few years, but as is typical in the music scene, new bands came in to replace the old ones.

"Where's Charlie planning on going?" Roscoe asked Nate.

"I've heard a lot of rumblings from the band members that they are not making enough money to stick with this gig," Nate said.

"Well, there are plenty of people who would join this band if people left."

"I know, Roscoe, but the chemistry the band has is key. You could bring a new bass player in every day, but no one would know what that person is going to do."

"I could find a bass player in ten minutes if I had to."

"Well, if you think that, Roscoe, why don't you find those people?"

"Why are you being such an ass?"

"Because Charlie is trying to get clean, and he is leaving the band because you have made this into a den of inequity."

"Den of what?"

"You need to go to college."

"And you need to go on a diet," Roscoe said as he chuckled.

"Look, Roscoe, we may have to cancel some gigs!"

"Come on, bass players are a dime a dozen."

Nate tossed Roscoe a dime and said, "Okay, start lining them up."

"No problem. I have a couple friends who have been wanting to play with us."

"Great. Are they users or dealers?"

"Up yours, fat man."

"Wow, maybe we could have the entire band pass out at the same time, that would be a first."

"Well, we have to rest sometime."

"I have a better idea. Why don't you sell horse right off the stage."

"Oh, I love that song!"

"What the America song?"

"Yeah."

"No wonder you worship that junk!"

"Well, if you want to talk about worship, look in the mirror! Junk food and a lot of it. Now that is worship."

"Hey, Roscoe, let's face it, if it weren't for me, you would be dead a long time ago."

Roscoe sat and starred at him as his mind went back over the years and the many trips to the emergency rooms all over the country. Then he shook his head and looked at the ground as he had a sudden realization.

"Hey, Nate…"

"Yeah, what?"

"Thanks."

Both of the men stood there looking at the ground. Then Roscoe spoke. "Look, Nate… I'm done."

"You quitting too?"

"No, I'm done with the junk. I want to go clean. I need your help."

Nate was blindsided by this reversal and just stood there in silence trying to process what he had just heard.

"Uh, okay. Well, let's work on this. You know you will have to go to meetings constantly, and I am going to be doing random drug tests."

Nate threw him a couple more challenges to test Roscoe's resolve. But he was steadfast in trying to get clean. However, he failed several times and each time came crawling back to Nate.

2005

Roscoe sat in the house with Liz, and he started humming a song and at the same time he was hammering away on the notes on the make-believe piano. Then he started saying, "La la la la la."

It was just a microcosm of a tune, but Liz remembered the tune, and she started humming along with him.

CHAPTER 19

1990

Eli walked into the playground and started playing on the jungle gym. Suddenly, he was surrounded by four big fifth graders. He didn't know what to do so he decided to try and befriend them.

"Hi, guys," he said.

"Hey, Eli. I want your lunch money."

"But I won't be able to eat today."

"Tough. Give it to me, or we are going to beat you up."

The group moved in closer. Eli sensing impending disaster suddenly heard a static-like noise in his brain. He had never heard this before, and he wasn't sure what it meant. Shortly after that, he started to feel rage building up inside of him. He lashed out at the main bully, and in the next second, four big fifth graders were pummeling him from every direction of the compass. He crumbled into a heap and then he felt hands going into his pockets and they left with everything he had. But to his great relief, he still had his life.

He was in pain for the rest of the day, and by the time he got home for the day, he was lightheaded because he was so hungry. From that day on, he tried to work on anything that would improve his self-defense. And the static noises in his brain kept happening, but they only happened when he was being threatened.

That's when Eli started lifting weights, clandestinely at first, and then he joined a gym and he was there every day for years. He also had multiple protein drinks each day. Then when the age of steroid use came around, he was one of the first in line, and his muscles started to develop astronomically. Working out became nothing less than an addiction for Eli, and if he missed a day, he would go through withdrawal. In addition to that, his temperament went downhill in a hurry, and he developed a nasty steroid rage. He lost many girlfriends, and guys couldn't even look at him sideways without setting him off. Eventually, he became a gym rat and that led to a job there and in the evenings, he worked at a couple bars. But with his temper, he had to move around a lot. Early on, he started taking aikido lessons, too, because he figured he would run into a martial arts aficionado eventually.

He could have a different woman every night, and with his new temper, he just about needed a new one every night. They were usually bartenders, then when he met Liz, who was singing at the bar where he was working. He became her bodyguard after he took out her previous boyfriend, who was treating her badly.

But unfortunately for Eli, the money he made did not pay his bills. He needed more, and he needed it now. By this time, he was an imposing man, solid muscle and with good control of martial arts. Eli knew he could pull this off, but when he walked into a bank that he had never been in before, as he walked around, he noticed every camera that was looking at him.

A bank manager walked up to him and asked, "Can I help you, sir?"

"Yes, I need a loan for a new car. Can you help me with that?"

"Yes, sir. I will have you talk to a loan officer."

"Officer? Is he a cop?"

"No, sir. That is just his title," the manager replied, but now Eli was on his radar. After talking to the loan officer for about a half an hour, during which time he scanned the entire place, he decided this was a no-go. He ended up walking out with no more money that he walked in with and then thought, *I am going to have to look someplace else for some extra cash.*

As he walked down the street, he saw someone leaving a house. The person didn't turn around and lock the door. That got Eli thinking.

THE GATE WAS OPEN

I wonder how many people leave their places unlocked? he pondered. He went home and called a bouncer friend of his.

"Hey, Jimmy, what ya doin' tonight?"

"Well, it's Monday, so no work for a few days, so I guess I'm slumming it."

"Yeah, me too. I could really use some more dough cause I can barely cover my bills. Well, I have an idea. Why don't you and me roll a house and see what we can come up with? You know, a little extra spending money."

"What do you mean 'roll a house'?"

"You know, knock it off."

"Well, I think I know what you mean, but look, dude, my old lady is here. I'll come over your place and we can talk," Jimmy said in a whisper.

Fifteen minutes later, Jimmy knocked on Eli's door and then the plans started in earnest.

"Dude, look, this will be easy. Just put some black clothes on and walk down a street, and when we see a house that has no lights on, we will just go around to the back and check for open doors," Eli said.

"Yeah, but what about dogs, and what about guns?"

"What about them? We will knock on the front door. If the dogs bark, that's a no-go. If someone comes to the door, that's a no-go."

"Well, when are we going to get started?"

"Let's just drive down the street tonight and see if we can spot any places."

"Well, what if we get caught?"

"Look at us. We look like two Mr. Universe candidates. If anybody faces off with us, we will kick their asses. And if they throw us in jail, we will own that place."

"Yeah, I guess."

"Okay. See you back here at nine."

"Okay, just don't say anything to the wife. she will freak out."

"What? I was going to put up posters all over town letting everyone know what we are doing?"

"Shut up!"

"You shut up. It's just you and me!"

"Okay. See you at nine."

The two met at nine and climbed into Eli's old Chevy and started driving up and down the streets of their neighborhood. They saw a lot of potential targets, and then they pulled into a grocery parking lot. Jimmy started taking his shoes off.

"What are you doing?"

"My feet sweat when I get nervous."

"We haven't done anything yet."

"Yet, but we are about to commit a crime."

"Well, what are your armpits doing?"

"Nothing. It's just my feet."

"Okay, well, let's just do this one, and if it seems too risky, then we won't do anymore."

"I always wanted to be a cop."

"Great. Well then, you will know when the cops are coming."

"Well, that would make me a mind reader."

"Yeah, not likely. Your brain is empty,"

"Yeah, and I suppose you are a genius."

"Well, who is running this show?"

"Come on. Let's get this over with."

The two walked down the street until they saw the darkened house. They tried the door and it opened. They slipped into the kitchen. They had a flashlight but didn't want to use it to avoid detection. Instead, they just let their eyes adjust to the darkness, and then they were able to move around with some difficulty.

"Oww! Shit!" Jimmy said in a muted shout.

"What the hell are you doing? You are going to get us killed."

"I stepped on a toy or something."

"Yeah, but your feet aren't sweating."

"Why don't you stick it where the sun don't shine?"

"Because you might step on it."

"Up yours!"

"Man, you are hung up with your ass. We are like the Keystone Cops."

"Maybe we are the Keystone Robbers?"

They walked slowly around the house, looking on counters for any money that had been left out. They looked into closets, and eventually, they found a gun closet and took a few guns out of it. In the end, they only came up with twenty bucks. Then they shoved the guns into their pockets, and Eli slid the barrel of a shotgun down his pant leg so it wasn't as obvious. When they got back to the car, Jimmy looked at the bottom of his foot with the flashlight.

"Couldn't you tell it was bleeding?"

"No, I thought it was just sweat."

"Well, don't worry. When they run your DNA, you will always have a place on the Keystone Cops."

"If we get caught, I'll never to be able to get a job as a cop."

"What do you mean 'we'? They won't have my DNA."

"Dude, you got me into this!"

"Yeah, but you had to leave a calling card. Maybe we should have just called the cops and told them what we were doing."

Years later, Eli and Jimmy quit robbing houses because they were no good at being cat burglars. Then Eli met Liz, and she had her mother's house, which was paid off, so when he moved in with her, that reduced his bills considerably. All Eli had to do was convince Liz that she needed a bodyguard. So he definitely didn't have to be robbing houses anymore.

2005

Eli and Liz had been together for five years and it had been a little rocky at times, but Eli would always pull the authoritarian act. That's what he had learned in childhood, and it had served him well. Liz accepted that because she was intimidated very easily. She had lost her mother at age ten and was always afraid of the sky falling. Even though he didn't act violently around her, Liz always thought that the potential was there. The World Trade Center coming down caused even more anxiety in Liz, and she hung closer to Eli. Eli, on the other hand, was ready to take on the world. He often got into fights with people in bars. If anyone came into his bar that even slightly looked like a terrorist, he would get in their face and see if he could provoke something. Everyone was on edge after the attack. Then Roscoe came into the picture, and Eli felt like he was being pushed out. That was not true, but Liz had to focus a lot of her attention on Roscoe and less on Eli.

CHAPTER 20

2005

Having heard Roscoe sing and attempt to play his fake piano inspired Liz to start singing again when they were in the house alone and the house was quiet. They sang songs from the sixties, seventies and eighties. Liz was stunned most of the time that this seventy-year-old man, who could hardly remember how to find the bathroom or even what her name was, could remember fifty song lyrics. But as soon as some music started or even some chords being strummed, he would come alive and almost as if by miracle, he would sing and went passionately at his keyboard. Unfortunately, she didn't have a piano and tried to think of some other sources but came up empty on that front too. For now, he would have to continue playing on the place mats and maybe forever.

Roscoe could hardly walk, so Liz had a hard time getting him out of the house, and she had to concentrate on things like walkers and wheelchairs that would make his life easier. Liz had to go to the mall, and she had to drag Roscoe along with her because of the incident with the basement stairs, and it would be better for both of them to get out of the house. Liz had her eye on a pair of comfy walking shoes that she needed for work. She knew they sold them in the shoe store at the mall.

She was walking hand-in-hand with Roscoe because she was afraid he might wander off. Then once they had entered the mall, Roscoe got distracted and broke free of her grip.

"Okay, but you stay right behind me," Liz said to the elderly man.

Liz kept looking over her shoulder as she passed store after store. Then she passed a big pretzel store.

"Hey, Roscoe, do you want a pretzel?" she asked.

He smiled and walked over to her, and she bought him a pretzel. Once he was content, she started walking through the mall again. She passed another eatery, a music store that had a number of instruments in it, and a sexy lingerie—which tempted Liz but she didn't dare enter that place with Roscoe in tow. Then she passed an outdoor store, and that's when she spied the shoe store up ahead. She momentarily forgot about her world as she zeroed in on her targeted item.

As she started into the store, she quickly looked behind to see if he still was happily munching on his pretzel. She saw nothing and froze in her tracks. But a feeling of guilt and anxiety rushed up from her solar plexus into her throat. Roscoe was nowhere to be seen. She started hyperventilating a little but quickly got it under control.

I can't lose control… Where did he go? she thought. She just stood there and scanned the mall hoping to spot the older man with the pretzel in his hand amongst all the kids. She began to panic a bit when she saw nothing she recognized. Then she started walking back the way she had come. She also had to walk into all the stores she had passed because he may have ducked into one of them. But her efforts were unsuccessful, and she was getting desperate. That's when she spotted a mall security guard. She walked quickly over to the guard.

"Excuse me, sir."

"Yes, ma'am."

"Um, I lost my dad."

"Excuse me?"

"I brought my dad to the mall, and I looked away for a second and he was gone."

The security guard stifled a laugh, then said, "Well, ma'am, that's the first time I've heard that one."

"Pardon me?"

"Well, ma'am, your dad is supposed to lose you."

"I know. It's complicated. He has Alzheimer's and sometimes he will just wander off."

"Oh, I'm sorry, ma'am, I wasn't trying to be disrespectful."

"Yeah, no problem. I just need help finding him because he can't take care of himself."

Liz and the guard were at an intersection where the four arms of the mall came together.

"Okay, so which direction did you come from?"

"I walked past that shop, so I came from that direction," Liz said pointing at the sexy lingerie shop.

The guard chuckled and nodded his head as he thought things he wasn't supposed to think.

"Well, can you give a description of your dad?"

"He is wearing a blue jacket and khaki trousers and a black cap."

"Okay, well, I will head down the arm that you came in."

"Then I will start down the arm that we were headed for," Liz said.

"Okay, I will contact my partners and get them started down the other arms."

As the guard started off looking, he walked by a crowd of people who were gathered around a musician playing at the piano store. The crowd caused him to veer out away from the store, and he was scanning all around for an older man with a blue top and khaki pants. Some of the people were dancing and some just stood and watched the hired pianist.

It was a common thing for music stored especially in malls to hire people to play and hopefully attract some customers in to look at the instruments. As Liz looked down the arm in the mall that she was assigned to, she became increasingly desperate.

Damn, I should have kept a hold of his hand instead of worrying about a pair of shoes, she thought. *He is no different than a three-year-old. I would have been a terrible mom.*

Then she caught herself because he constantly referred to her as Mom.

No, I am a terrible caretaker, she pondered.

She got to the end of her arm in the mall and walked out into the sunshine and out of her frustration she started yelling, "Roscoe!"

Then she turned to face another direction and yelled again, "Roscoe!"

People around her turned to look at the young woman who was letting out gut-wrenching screams. Then Liz dropped to her knees and started wailing, and she put her face in her hands mostly to hide her embarrassment.

"Ma'am, are you okay?" a young man said.

Liz couldn't talk because of the uncontrollable crying. She just kept shaking her head.

"Do you want me to call someone for you?"

"No, I lost my dad," Liz said.

"Oh, I am so sorry, ma'am," the young man said and typical of many men he didn't know what to say next. "Is there anything I can help you with?"

"Well, you could find my dad."

"Oh, I thought your dad had passed away."

"Ah no, but he has lost his mind, and I turned around for a second and he was gone!"

"Oh, well, you should notify the security guards."

"I did, and they are looking too."

"Well, I would be willing to help, too, if you need more eyes."

"No, that's okay. At some point, he will turn up. I just hope he doesn't get into any trouble or get hurt."

"Okay, well, I am going to go, then."

"Yes, you can go, and I'll go back inside and keep looking."

"Okay, good luck!"

"Thank you so much for your kindness."

"No problem."

Liz walked back into the mall wiping away tears and smearing her mascara. And now that some time had passed, she thought she might get lucky. As she walked through the mall, she looked into every shop and talked to people in every one. But no one had seen him. Because many of the shops had bathrooms, she had to be sure that no stone was left unturned. As she approached the intersection of the mall, she saw the first security guard, and he was talking to another guard. She walked over to them.

"Hi, any luck?"

"No, ma'am. Haven't seen him yet. Is there anything you can tell us about him?"

"Well, he used to be a singer in a rock-and-roll band, but that was many years ago."

Suddenly Liz heard a song that was being played by the hired piano player. As she felt the goosebumps rise on her arms and the tiny hairs on the back of her neck standing on end, she looked over her shoulder and saw the crowd. She couldn't get through the group of people, but she could hear the ivories being tickled.

"Excuse me," she said as she tried to squirm through the crowd.

"Excuse—" Liz's mouth dropped open.

Roscoe had the look on his face of complete abandonment, and even more astonishing was the fluidity of the man's hands. He had played as if he was twenty-five-years old. That brought another round of tears to Liz. She walked over to Roscoe and put her hand on his shoulder. he looked up at Liz.

"Hi, Mom. Look what I found!," Roscoe said.

She smiled through her tears and then remembered she used to sing. She stood by the piano and whispered in his ear. A smile came across his face, and he started pounding out the notes. Liz stood beside Roscoe and cleared her throat. Then she began to sing in a very melodic and deep way. She was singing her favorite song and that inspired Roscoe even more.

He continued playing and Liz and Roscoe were singing in a duet for the first time. Their voices had a very unique twist of both youth and age. And this was with virtually no practice. Roscoe's voice was still pretty smooth, and most impressive was he could still remember the notes on the piano and he could belt out the songs. Just like the old days.

They continued playing for a few hours. The security guards walked by, and Liz waved them over and when they walked up to Liz, the conversation started.

"Hi, look who I found!"

"Hiding in plain sight!" the security guard said.

Liz could laugh with abandon now the crisis was over.

"I want to thank you so much for your help with my problem."

"No problem, ma'am."

"By the way, you two would make a great group, are you professionals?

"Professional what?" Roscoe asked.

"Well, singers."

"Not yet, but thank you."

CHAPTER 21

2005

The day was young, and Liz walked hand-in-hand with Roscoe to the shoe store in the mall. She got the shoes she needed. Then they went home, and they hummed all the way home. Liz tried to come up with a solution for getting a piano for Roscoe. That unfortunately was an impossibility, but she couldn't have him pounding away on the place mat.

The next day, Liz took Roscoe back to the mall, and when they got to the musical instrument store, Roscoe inquired, much like a three-year-old would have, "Can I play again, Mom?"

"Not today, Roscoe."

"Why not?"

"I want to look for something else."

They walked into the store until they were approached by a salesman.

"Oh, it is the duet from yesterday."

"Yes, I want to apologize if we caused any problems yesterday," Liz said.

"Are you kidding? We had the best sales day we had in a long time."

"Well, good," she said with a smile on her face.

"Are you two a group, like Jack and Janelle?" he said indicating a popular group in the current music scene.

"No, we aren't as good as they are. I think they have had a few number-one hits, haven't they?"

"Well, I think you should give it a try. With a little practice, you could be on the top of the charts."

"Actually, this guy was on the top of the charts when he was younger."

"Really? What's your name, sir?"

Roscoe just stood there smiling and the only thing that came out of his mouth was, "Yeah, yeah, yeah," and he gave the salesman a thumbs up.

The salesman was confused and kind of sensed that Roscoe was mentally challenged. He looked at Liz, and she spoke up, "He has dementia."

"No way!"

Liz just stood there nodding her head. "Yup."

"And this is the same guy that was playing yesterday?"

"Yes, it is."

"You have got to be kidding me, this has got to be some kind of a world record."

"I don't know," Liz replied.

"Hey, can you wait here? I think someone wants to talk to you."

They stood there for a minute, and the sales man came back with another man.

"Ma'am, this is Rick. He's the manager of this store."

"Hi, Rick."

"Hi, what is your name?"

"I am Liz, and this is Roscoe."

"Roscoe… Roscoe Gillette?"

"The one and the same," Liz replied.

"What was the group he used to play with?"

"The Backdoor Brothers," Liz said.

"I remember them. They were one of my favorite bands when I was younger," the older graying man said. "I can't believe you are in my shop."

"Well, I came back in to look for an instrument for him."

"That's fantastic," Rick said. "What are you looking for?"

"Well, I would like a piano, but I couldn't afford one of those."

"I think I have the answer for you."

THE GATE WAS OPEN

"Oh?"

"This piano is only $2600."

"No, you don't understand. I can't afford that much."

"Well, I have a used stand-up piano for $1,500."

"I'm sorry, but Roscoe and I are on a tight budget."

"Okay. Well, look, I can order you an electronic keyboard for $300."

"And that's all I would need to spend?"

"Well, you need a strand to hold the keyboard and a bench to sit on."

"And how much are those?"

"About one hundred and fifty."

"Yeah, this is getting a little out of control, and I can tell this will be too difficult for me to handle with the budget I am on."

"Oh, okay," the manager said with a frown on his face.

"I'll just walk around and look at what there is in the store," Liz said.

"Okay."

"Come on, Roscoe," she said.

As they walked around the store looking at the exorbitant prices, Roscoe asked, "Can we play again, Mom?"

"No, Roscoe. Let's head home, and we will practice singing some songs."

They started walking out of the store.

"Pardon me, Liz and Roscoe," they heard from behind.

"Hi, Rick," Liz said to the manager.

"You know, I have an idea."

"Okay, what's that?"

"We day a terrific day yesterday probably the best day we have had in a long time."

"Oh, well, great. I'm glad we could help out."

"So what I am thinking if you and Roscoe could come and perform every weekend and I will give you a cut off everything we make on those days."

"Wow, that's a great idea because I have been thinking that we might be able to make money doing this."

"Then you could have enough money to buy a keyboard or even a piano."

"Well, that's a win-win for us because we could work on new songs, and we could make a lot of people happy."

"And we will make a lot of money," Rick said. "Don't forget about that!"

"Yes, of course. As I said before, it would be a win-win, so everybody would make out well."

"Well, let's say next weekend then, okay?"

"Yes, that would work, but at least at first, I only want Roscoe playing for four hours."

"That's fine," Rick said.

As they were driving home, Liz couldn't contain her excitement.

"Roscoe, we got a job! Or should I say we got a gig."

Roscoe just sat there in silence and then he smiled. When they got home, Eli was in the kitchen fixing lunch.

"Eli, guess what?"

"Ahh, what?"

"Roscoe and I got our first gig."

"Where?"

"In the mall," she said, nearly jumping up and down.

"You two are going to work in the mall? Doing what?"

"Roscoe and I went to the mall, and he started playing a piano and singing and then we both started singing and the manager said we could play there every weekend!"

"How much are they going to pay you?"

"Well, after a little while they are going to give Roscoe a keyboard."

Eli just stood there dumbfounded.

"So nothing then," he said.

"Yeah, but if we get started at the mall, we will be able to start booking gigs."

"Liz, you are letting them walk all over you. You are working for free!"

"I am not!"

"Liz, don't be stupid!"

"I'm not stupid. If you would have seen Roscoe's face come alive and his fingers were playing all over that keyboard!"

"Well, I will have to see that to believe it."

"If we start doing gigs, we will need someone to carry the equipment."

"What are you forgetting about all the money Roscoe has in every bank in this country?"

"No, but we can't access his accounts. They won't let us!"

"So your solution is to just perform for free. Wow, that's a great idea!"

Eli stood up and looked sideways at the old man sitting at the kitchen table like a boiled potato. The harsh words made Roscoe tear up and he walked into a corner.

"Oh, great, Liz. Now he is crying,"

"Damn it, Eli. You hurt his feelings!"

"Jesus, Liz. Is he an old man or a three-year-old!"

"Eli, if you would have seen the transformation that I just saw you would have been stunned."

"That's unlikely. There's nothing I haven't seen."

Liz walked over and hugged Roscoe. "It's okay, Roscoe. We will be okay."

Roscoe walked back to the table and Liz handed him one of his favorite placemats. Roscoe immediately started playing an unknown tune, then she glanced at Eli who was staring at the hands flying over the keys. Liz just watched as Eli got this look of astonishment on his face. Then Eli stared shaking his head.

"Yeah, but there is no sound. How could that be so amazing?"

"I'm telling you that I watched him play a real piano. This guy is a professional."

"Huh," he said with a snort of derision.

Liz looked at Roscoe who just sat there and smiled at her. Eli shook his head, not really buying the story that was being handed to him.

1987

The ten-year-old Liz was crushed her mother had just died. Liz had become a caregiver, a nurse, a bill-payer, a cook, a housekeeper, and a general do it all. Then one day, she walked into her mom's bedroom, and she could immediately sense the difference. A stillness hung in the air, and she wasn't sure if it was an odor or a feeling or a sense. But Liz knew.

"Mother?" she said in barely a whisper. There was no response.

"Mother?" she said with much more volume. Liz was hoping that Becky would wake up and yell at her for waking up the sleeping mother. She was ready to beg for forgiveness, but there was no response, and then she felt the hairs standing on the back of her neck.

"Mootheerr!" the young girl screamed, then she collapsed in tears. But she couldn't just stay on the carpet. She suddenly snapped into action and ran to her mother. Liz was too young for a first aid course, and she doesn't know CPR. She shook the rigid body, hoping that her mother would spring to life. Suddenly, her senses came back to life and she started observing things. A close look at her mom's face, and Liz saw the bluish skin. Liz tried to move her arm but it was frozen in place. She clutched her mom's face in her hands, and it was cold to the point that she recoiled from the feeling. There was a slight odor of stool in the room. That made Liz vomit into her mouth, and the taste of acid from the stomach contents was too much, so she spat the substance out on the carpet. It took a while, but eventually, Liz accepted the obvious. Her mother was not there anymore.

CHAPTER 22

1987

After Becky's demise, Liz was a ten-year-old with at least as much experience as most adults. She didn't know what to do with her mom's death because death was one thing she had yet to deal with. She picked up the phone and dialed 911 and explained to the operator that she needed an ambulance. The operator asked if her mother was still breathing, and Liz started to cry.

"Ma'am, I just told you that my mom just died, and the only thing you can say is, is she breathing?"

"My apologies, honey, but we have to ask these questions."

"Just send whoever you have to send."

"They are on the way."

The rest of the day was a constant stream of officials. First, the ambulance arrived, then the police arrived, then the coroner. When the police officer was there, he realized that Liz was alone, and there were no other adults around. When Liz was questioned, the police officer found out that there was no father and no aunts, uncles, grandparents or anyone to take responsibility for this child. Social Services was contacted, and at the end of the day, a woman showed up. The body had long since departed, and she was very kind, but Liz didn't like where the conversation went.

"Hi, Liz. My name is Rose."

"Hi, Rose. What are you here for?"

"I'm with social services, and because you are alone now, the state has a responsibility to take care of you."

"But I can take care of myself."

"Yes, a lot of young people think they can handle everything themselves."

"Well, my mother had a brain tumor, and I took care of her for the last two years."

"That's impressive, but there are certain laws in this country, and we need to abide by those!"

"So what happens then?"

"Well, we have to find you a foster family, and you will move in with them."

"But my mom paid the house off, and I am in the will to get the house, so I am going to stay here!"

"I'm sorry, Liz, but I am afraid that will be impossible."

"Why is it impossible?"

"Well, there are other bills that you have to pay when you have a house."

"And I have been paying those for two years."

"Yes, Liz, but there are still the laws of this state that we have to follow."

Liz dropped into a funky mood as she realized that even though she was right, the social worker was not going to let Liz have her way.

"Well, what am I going to do with this house if I can't live here?"

"I am not an expert on houses because I am a social worker, but another thing you should be thinking about is the state may try and seize this house out from under you, so possibly the best thing you can do is get an attorney."

"Well, shit. That sucks. So what is the next step?"

"I am going to turn you over to child protective services. They are very kind, and they will take good care of you until you get into the foster care system."

"Yeah, but you don't understand. I don't want to be in the foster care system."

"You know, Liz, a lot of kids do very well in the foster care. They thrive, but you can't fight it."

"And a lot of kids haven't had to care for a dying parent, and it really sucks when you lose your only parent and then are penalized for it. How can the laws of this state be so cruel?" Liz said with tears streaming down her face. "I am way more advanced than most kids!"

"I can see that."

2005

Lis walked into the bedroom and Eli was sleeping.

"Eli," she whispered.

"Eli," she said in a louder voice as she stroked his shoulder.

"Hey," Eli shouted as he erupted into a rage.

"Jesus, take it easy. All I was doing was caressing you."

"What! Why are you waking me? I had a late night last night!"

"I'm sorry, but I have a doctor's appointment can you watch Roscoe till get back?"

"Can't you take him with you?"

"No, I have an ob-gyn appointment."

"Well, can't you take him to a doctor and drop him off while you are at your OB whatever appointment?"

"Come on, Eli. I rarely ask for your help. This is the doctor that takes care of my ovaries.

"What's wrong with you?"

"I'm just having a little pain in my lady parts."

"What are your lady parts?"

"I think it's my ovaries."

"Well, I'm very tired. I had a long night," he said as he yawned a long yawn.

"Please, baby. I don't ask all that much from you."

"Well, he's a musical genius, but he can't even get dressed by himself."

"What? He's dressed."

"Never mind. I'll watch him."

"Thank you, sweetie." Then she turned to Roscoe an said, "Roscoe, don't leave Eli's sight, okay?"

Roscoe nodded in silence. Eli rolled over and fell back to sleep, but then he heard something crash to the floor.

"Roscoe!" Eli screamed, then he dragged himself out of the bed and staggered into the living room. Roscoe was standing there looking at a broken vase.

"What did you do?" Eli said.

"I don't know," Roscoe replied.

"Looks like you are ruining everything."

"Where did Mom go?"

"You crazy old man, you heard her. She said she was going to the doctor that takes care of the parts down there," he said, pointing at his crouch.

"There is something wrong down there," Roscoe said, grabbing his penis. Eli was stunned when he saw that.

"You see, I told you she should have taken you with her. Are you talking about Liz or yourself?"

Roscoe starred pulling his pants down.

"Dude! Don't be showing me that stuff!"

Roscoe had a confused look on his face and then he spoke.

"It's gotten small."

"What's gotten small?"

Roscoe pointed to his penis and said, "This."

"Dude, I don't want to talk about your junk!"

"But it's small."

"Well, it's called erectile dysfunction. It happens to a lot of guys."

"You?" Roscoe asked.

"No, not me. I am only thirty-eight!"

Eli walked into the kitchen and dropped down into a chair put his face in his hands and sighed a long sigh. He looked at Roscoe as he tried to wrap his brain around this weird situation that he found himself in now. Then he poured himself a cup of coffee. He walked back into the living room shaking his head.

"Roscoe, what would you do if Liz left you?"

"Who?"

"You know, Mom. Mom," Eli said as his volume was increased. "What if Mom wasn't here to take care of you?"

Roscoe starred tearing up but just sat there speechless.

"What's that? That's what I thought. Nothing upstairs," Eli said as he stared at Roscoe.

Then Roscoe raised his right hand, with his index finger against his temple and his thumb pointing up to the sky to give the symbol of a hand gun.

"What? What the fuck?" Eli shouted. "Are you saying that you would off yourself?"

Then Eli got up and ran into the bedroom and found his Glock 9mm handgun. Then he hid it in a dresser drawer and then walked back into the living room. His mind started to run wild, and then he realized that the burden that Roscoe had put into his happy little world might have an easy solution. Now he thought he might have a way out of this mess, but he had to separate himself from all of this.

Liz came home about an hour later and Eli was dozing off on the couch and Roscoe wasn't anywhere to be seen.

"Oh no. Oh no!" Liz said.

"What's wrong now?" Eli said.

"Where's Roscoe?"

"I think he's napping in the spare bedroom."

Liz walked into the spare bedroom and the stress flowed out of her when she saw Roscoe lying supine on the bed. She exhaled audibly and then she tried to slip out of the bedroom without waking him but was unsuccessful.

"Mom?"

"Hi, Roscoe. I'm Liz," she said, always trying to break this unending confusion.

He swung his feet of the bed but wasn't able to put his shoes on. Liz couched down and helped him with his shoes. Then he walked back out to the living room.

"How did it go with Roscoe?"

"You won't believe it! He told me he has erectile dysfunction."

"What? You didn't talk to him about having sex did you?"

"Noooo!" Eli said, chuckling.

"You better not have, and Roscoe doesn't even know what that word means."

"I have no interest in talking to the old man about sex."

"That would be like talking to a three-year-old, and it would be totally inappropriate."

"Come on the obviously has had sex before," Eli said, pointing in her direction.

"So exactly how did this conversation go?" Liz inquired.

"He started it," Eli said.

"Yeah, right. Roscoe started a conversation about sex."

"He said his penis had gotten smaller so I figured he was talking about erectile dysfunction. But then he asked me if I had it, and I made sure that he understood that I was all man, right, Liz?"

"Well, how would I know that? And you better not have made fun of him."

"No, but it's all good. But I am not gay, and I don't talk to guys about their junk.

"And by the way, Eli, I made out fine too."

"Well, I was going to ask about you."

"Yeah right," she said.

"Well, what did your girl doctor say?"

"My gynecologist said I still have polycystic ovarian syndrome."

"Well, you left me in the dust with that one."

"That's the condition I have in my ovaries, and at least for now, is preventing pregnancy."

"Well, that's not bad. We can still do the you-know-what, can't we?"

"Eli, you are such an idiot."

"What are you talking about? I love you!"

"You love one part of me, but I think that's it."

"Maybe we should talk about Roscoe's penis," he said with a grin on his face.

"Why don't you shut up!"

"Calm down."

"Don't tell me to calm down. That's disrespectful."

Liz put her arm through Roscoe's arm and they walked out.

"Where are we going, Mom?"

"We are going to the mall so we can have fun!"

1987

Liz checked into the first foster home with the woman from child protective services. Even though she was only ten years old, she had the maturity of a much older woman. That was followed by a succession of foster homes. When Liz entered a foster home and realized she could take care of things better than her foster parents, things went downhill from there. Liz ran away from three foster homes. She got good at dodging and dealing with law enforcement.

That's when Liz found herself in a bar on open mic night. The bartender called the cops as soon as he noticed an underage in his bar. But the time the cops got arrived, Liz had found the microphone and she lowered it to her level and she was belting out songs to where the patrons in the bar were stunned by this singer. That's when a couple guys were taking an interest in the young girl singing on stage, and a female dancer quickly intervened to protect the aspiring singer. After that, she told Liz she would buy her dinner, and they went to a restaurant.

When a law enforcement officer got to the bar and Liz was gone, the bartender said he heard them talking about going to Dotty's diner to get something to eat. The officer was running out of patience, and when he got to Dotty's, he found Liz and her protector and then he called child protective services. The same woman from before showed up again and said hello to Liz and thanked the dancer for helping out. Then she contacted another foster home, and Liz ended up in the foster care system again.

CHAPTER 23

2005

The true meaning of *animas* in the dictionary is a strong feeling of dislike or hate. Another definition is a usually prejudiced and often spiteful and malevolent ill will. Eli Animas was all of these things times one hundred. He was the personification of evil and the manifestation of wrong. Unfortunately for Liz, she didn't see his brain squirming like a bag of snakes as Eli began to scheme the dishonest plan to eliminate the current problem in his life. Roscoe had caused a lot of angst in Eli's mind and his very childlike bullying approach to everything in life. He often used his physical strength to get what he wanted, thus the definition of bullying.

Liz worked at the laundry facility where they did personnel laundry for individuals as well as laundry for hotels and other organizations, such as a football team. A Hispanic member of the staff was talking to Liz and the topic came to husbands and Liz mentioned that her boyfriend's name was Eli Animas. When she said that the woman turned pale, and it was obvious that she was afraid of something.

"What's wrong, Sofia?"

"*Perida garra, este hombre es satan!*"

"I am sorry, but I don't speak Spanish."

Sofia just stood there shaking her head. Then she said, "The name Animas means 'lost soul.'"

Hispanic people are extremely religious, and when someone possesses a lost soul, they believe this may be the home of the devil.

THE GATE WAS OPEN

And Sofia started walking away from Liz because she thought that the devil may be with her. Liz just finished her shift at the laundry company, but the words had hit her with a lot of power. The laundry company always had the odor of detergent, and lint from the dryers had its own strange smell. The sound of the constant droning of the machines was hard on the ears, so Liz wore headphones with music playing in them to learn new songs. And without a lot of extraneous sound, Liz was able to escape into her own private world. Liz hated the feeling of lint and dust which seemed to settle on everything; it was most disturbing on her exposed skin. But the workplace was too hot to wear long-sleeved garments.

After this day, she now thought that it was a good time to depart from Eli, now that she had a lot of responsibility with Roscoe. But she was terrified to broach this topic with Eli because she knew it might just be the straw that breaks the camel's back and sets him into to a rage.

None of the workers would talk to her for the rest of the day.

As Liz drove home, she knew she would have to face Eli because this was a down day for him. And when she walked through the door, she had no idea what she would get from him. She was still clinging to the idea that he was Satan reincarnate. And that made her very nervous as she walked up to the door of the house. She dropped her keys as she tried to unlock the door and the tiny hairs on the back of her neck stood on end.

When she entered the house, Eli was still unconscious on the couch and Roscoe was standing in front of the thermostat and he turned it up and then he looked at his watch. The Rolex logo made him smile. He turned the thermostat down and then looked at his watch again. Then he started counting the numbers on the face of the watch. After this episode, he looked at the blank wall and with his right index finger, seemed to be counting the numbers in an imaginary circle. Roscoe had a significant amount of hearing loss so he didn't hear Liz coming in, and Eli was out on the couch. She walked around the couch and was afraid to touch Roscoe, for fear that the shock might stop his heart. Instead, she walked to the side of him to try and catch his attention.

"Mom!" he said in an excited voice.

"I'm Liz, and you are my father, but I am not your mother."

He smiled and laughed a small laugh.

"Where were you?" he asked.

"I was at work, but do you remember what we were going to do this weekend?"

Roscoe just stared at her but couldn't come up with the answer. He started to get a sad look on his face.

"Oh, don't worry, buddy. I will help you out," she said.

"I have to go to the bathroom."

"Well, Roscoe, the bathroom is right there," she replied, pointing at the open door.

"He said I couldn't," Roscoe whispered.

"Who? Eli?"

Hearing his name, Eli roused from his slumber. "Hey, you're home."

"Are you telling Roscoe he can't use the bathroom?" Liz said as her tone rose.

"Well, every day, the guy does something even crazier than the day before."

"What happened today?"

"So he tells me he has to take a crap. And I said, well, go ahead."

"And?" Liz said impatiently.

"He goes into the bathroom, and when he's finished, he walks out. About an hour later, I needed to take a leak, and when I walked into the bathroom, there were all these used toilet papers neatly folded into about four-inch squares. He was saving them for something!"

"You know, I never know when you are telling the truth. Yesterday, it was his penis; today, it is his ass."

"Not his ass! His shit!"

"So then what happened?"

"I made him go back in there and throw them in the toilet. And he immediately started crying like a three-year-old!"

"You made him feel bad!" Liz exclaimed.

"Damn right, I made him feel bad. When I was in elementary school, one of my classmates would stick his finger up his nose and eat his boogers. And the teacher made him stop because it was gross. Just like this psycho activity with the toilet paper."

"Eli, there are better ways to change Roscoe's behavior other than corporal punishment that you keep doling out."

"Oh yeah, shake his hand."

"What do you mean shake his hand?"

"You know reach out and shake his hand," Eli said and then grabbed Liz's arm and dragged her over to Roscoe.

"Eli, let go of my arm! You're hurting me!"

"Roscoe went to the corner and tried to hide from all the angry words.

"You see not so brave when you could be grabbing a handful of shit."

"Roscoe, go wash your hands, and make sure you wash your hands every time you use the bathroom."

Roscoe disappeared into the bathroom for a good ten minutes. Eli stormed out of the house and paced back and forth in front of the house while he smoked a cigarette and then two and then three. Liz knocked on the bathroom door, and when Roscoe opened it the aroma of stool was definitely heavy in the air. She grabbed a can of air freshener and filled the bathroom with a fine mist of pine scent that she felt settle on her face.

"Roscoe, are you okay?"

Roscoe nodded.

"Did Eli hurt you?"

Roscoe shook his head from side to side with a big frown on his face.

"Well, look you can't save your toilet paper. After you use it, it must go into the toilet—and I mean right after you use it, not five minutes later. Do you understand?"

Roscoe nodded with the frown still crossing his face, and the frown increased in length when he looked into the toilet bowl.

Eli walked back into the house and plopped back down on the couch.

"Liz, do think it is possible to die from this disease?" Eli asked.

"I'm sure it is."

"Well, what do you die from? Do you forget to breathe?"

"No, you forget to live."

"Well, who was that guy at the hospital that was telling you all about this disease?"

"Oh, you mean John?"

"Yeah, the ass who kicked me out of the room when I should have stayed in the room!"

"You're right, Eli. I should go back and talk to John again and see if he can help me understand what's going on here."

After Eli put his two cents in, he went to the bar, even though it was his night off. He got very drunk at the bar, and he noticed that the female bar fly was back and threatening to do the same thing.

"Hey, bartender, she's going to do that face plant again," Eli sputtered out.

"Yeah. She does it every night." the bartender said. "And you are the bouncer, Eli, why don't you do something about it?"

"Not working tonight."

"Well, what are you doing?"

"Getting drunk."

"Well, I know that is a very difficult thing…but do you have to brag so much."

"Set me up again."

The bartender poured five shots and lined them up in front of Eli.

"There ya go, my friend."

"Now set up the rest of the bar."

"Okay."

The rest of the people sitting in the bar sent a lot of thanks in Eli's direction, as the shots hit the bar.

When he had tied one on, he staggered out to the parking lot and climbed into his car. But he couldn't remember which key he was supposed to use and got so pissed off, he started punching things inside the car. The driver's side window vaporized into tiny shards of glass. He made his way back into the bar and asked the bartender to call him a cab.

"That's a good idea!" the bartender said.

THE GATE WAS OPEN

He was leaning on the bar waiting for the cab when the woman at the other end of the bar fell off her stool and landed on her back. As she hit, the back of her head smacked the concrete, and the blood started to flow. Eli walked down to the unmoving woman and then grabbed her unconsumed shot and threw it back.

CHAPTER 24

2005

Eli was thirty-eight about a month ago. When he got out of the cab in front of the house and staggered to the front door, then sat down on the front step and leaned back until he was supine on the concrete stoop, he was asleep in about thirty seconds. Of course, *asleep* was a very nebulous word. Was he asleep or unconscious?

At eight in the morning, the heat of the sun was intense, and he sat up and looked at a sailboat out cruising in the Atlantic Ocean.

Yeah, that's what we are going to get when Liz gets that money, he thought.

He was very dizzy and thought back over his life. He had started drinking at age thirteen, and by eighteen, he had graduated his alcohol abuse to marijuana. He smoked a joint every morning to get his day started, and when he got to work, he sprayed some ozone in his mouth to eliminate the odor of pot. Then he walked into the bar and immediately threw back a shot. After that, he had to come down a little bit and swallowed a Quaalude, which calmed him down enough to keep him focused as a clean-up person in the bar. That regiment was especially needed when the bar floor was covered with vomit.

Eli stood up from the concrete stoop and spit out on the lawn. The heat was oppressive mostly because of the ninety percent humidity. He could smell the odor of his armpits, and the taste in his mouth was one of stomach acid. He brought up another phlegm ball from deep in his throat and spit it halfway out on the lawn. Then he turned around, and Liz was standing inside the storm door with her hands on her hips.

"Shit!" Eli said as she disappeared back into the house.

He shook his head trying to come up with a believable lie. Then he walked into the house and headed right to the bathroom to take a shower. When he walked out of the bathroom and back into the living room, he saw the note.

"Eli we need to have a talk," the note said.

Liz put Roscoe in the car, and she drove him to see John. John had a sign on the door that said, "Adult Protective Services."

"Hi, Liz," he said and then followed with, "Roscoe," in a very upbeat tone.

"Mom, who is this man?"

"How are you doing with the mom reference?" John asked her.

"I'm getting used to it, but it's just weird that he thinks I'm his mom."

"I understand," John said with a smile on his face.

"What causes Alzheimer's, John?"

"Well, it's hard to say. There is a lot of confusion surrounding the disease and its effects on the body."

"So there is no way to prevent the disease?"

"Well, I didn't say that, but if you're asking if there is a pill that you could take, I am sorry to say that the research has not caught up to that yet."

"So how do I prevent this in myself?"

"Well researchers think that a healthy diet and physical exercise help prevent it."

"Wow, that's about as general as saying, 'Take two aspirin and call me in the morning,'" she said.

"I agree. That's why I say that researchers are still working on it."

"Well, does drinking cause dementia?"

"There is evidence that alcohol abuse causes a disorder called Korsakoff's syndrome," John answered.

"Why all these weird names?"

"They are not weird names. The diseases are names after the researchers that discovered them."

"Well, this is getting complicated."

"Not really. It is just very frustrating for primary caregivers."

"Well, this is my dad, is it possible that I could get it too?"

"No, there is no evidence that this has any genetic predisposition."

"You could have just said no."

"What kind of things do you do together?"

"That's the exciting part, John," she said with a big smile.

"Exciting?"

"We went to a piano store, and Roscoe sat down and started playing song after song. And singing those songs too. Just like when he was young!"

"Wow, I have heard of this but never seen it myself."

"I am thinking of starting a musical group because I used to sing when I was young."

"Wow, Liz, that is incredible! And it would be very cool if your band worked out because it would be the first time that I or other scientists have ever heard of something like that."

"Really? So we are the firsts?"

"First time I have ever heard of someone coming out of a dementia diagnosis to play music!"

"Well, when you say coming out, I think that is a stretch."

"Yeah, and when you say it these days, it means something different."

"How is it possible that he could have these songs memorized but not even know the difference between me and my mother?"

"I'm telling you, Liz. It has never been seen before, at least not by me."

"Well, that is good because I thought I was losing my mind."

"So far I have not seen any signs of Alzheimer's in you, Liz."

"Hallelujah."

"Do you think you could get Roscoe to sing something?"

"Ah, maybe. Roscoe, let's sing a song for John."

Roscoe just sat there smiling. Nothing was uttered from his mouth. John just sat there with his arms crossed and watched as

Roscoe just looked at the floor. Liz started singing a song from the sixties. But Roscoe just continued smiling.

"I swear he can belt out the songs, both by voice and on the piano."

"Well, maybe he has stage fright."

"John, there were fifty people in the mall all gathered around him!"

"Hmm."

"Oh no. You don't think his Alzheimer's has taken a turn for the worse!"

"Well, there is a chance that this disease can get worse, than better and so on."

"Oh no."

"I'm going to do a test on him. Roscoe, I'm going to give you four words and want you to remember them. Are you ready?" Roscoe nodded his head. Then John said, "Apple, clarity, Mr. Robinson, and tank. Can you repeat them back to me?"

"I have no need for those words," Roscoe said.

Liz's head dropped into her open hand, and she did her best to hold the tears in.

"Well, how can we start a band if he has an off switch that he can use at any time?"

"Well, everyone has the freedom of free choice, so even though he has dementia, he still has the right to make decisions that affect him. And maybe being in a band is not in the cards for you two. Maybe you could go into senior residences. I know that would make them happy.

"Yeah, I just wish he didn't make a liar out of me."

"No, Liz, I believe you. He can sing and play the piano."

Liz and Roscoe left the hospital and just to make sure that he hadn't lost his abilities, Liz drove straight to the mall and walked directly to the music store. Roscoe's face beamed as he saw the pianos. He sat down at the keyboard and started tickling the ivories, slow at first, and Liz was surprised once again as Roscoe started playing classical music.

Liz then began to wonder if Roscoe was going to continue this on/off ability to perform. She knew that he had spent the majority of his young life playing music and wondered why he had this occasional disinterest in playing. Also, she had forced herself not to think about the white elephant in the room and that was Eli's drunkenness. She suddenly realized that she was dealing with two diseases, dementia and alcoholism—which could lead to the first disease.

When Liz walked into the house, Eli was in his typical unresponsive position on the couch. The door slamming closed brought him around to consciousness. And he knew he was on Liz's list of retribution.

"Hi, sweetie," Eli said.

Liz ignored the greeting and helped the door open for Roscoe. Eli sensed the anger and knew he had to change the subject quickly.

"Look, I was thinking about Roscoe."

Liz had a skeptical look on her face, but decided to respond anyway.

"You were thinking, that's a change."

"Look, Liz, you can be the biggest bitch in the world, but I am trying to help you out."

"Okay, what did you come up with?"

"Well, do you think it is possible to die from Alzheimer's?"

"Eli, we already talked about this. I'm not sure who's worse, you or Roscoe."

"Did we?"

"Yeah. Remember, you wondered if people could die from the lack of memory, and I said, 'What do they die from, forgetting to breathe?'"

"Oh?" Eli said with a look of confusion on his face.

"You know, let's change the topic you seem to be having early onset dementia."

"What?" Eli shouted. "Don't put this on me."

"I just learned that alcohol abuse can lead to something called Kor...sa...something. It's some guys name."

"That's bullshit, Liz. It's just old age."

"Well, how do some people live to one hundred years and still have a strong memory?"

"That doesn't happen!"

"Yes, it does."

"You are the one who is drunk," Eli stammered out.

"Shut up, and I know why you want to talk about dementia and death because you want Roscoe's money."

"Well, since he is your father, it sure would help you take care of him!"

"And buy that truck that you want!"

"Shit. Look, Liz, I am trying to help, but I keep on running into a brick wall with you."

"And I appreciate that, but you are always looking for the quick prize money. And I am looking for one thing and one thing only. And that is taking care of one person and that is the only relative that I have left."

"Okay, well, I will try to do better, but it would help you and Roscoe if you would have access to that money."

"I know, but the only one that has carte blanche access to that money is Roscoe, and the bank will step in the way if I try to get him to withdraw that money. The only thing that will give me access to his money…is his death," she said with a catch in her throat.

Eli didn't know what to do and reached out his hand to touch her shoulder but then removed his hand. Then he touched her shoulder again. Meanwhile, his mind was doing somersaults because of what Liz had just said: "his death." And that was why he was having trouble soothing her in her time of need.

CHAPTER 25

2005

She hated walking into bars because they were the dens of decadence. The only thing she could think of was immoral behavior in this place. It was early in the day, but there were still a few regulars sitting around the bar. The walls were covered by flashing signs advertising different brands of beer, and the air was thick with cigarette smoke. The sound of a jukebox played some old sixties songs. As Liz walked back into the depths of the dark bar, she felt the breeze of a ceiling fan which temporarily cleared the air. She leaned over the bar and asked the bartender a question.

"Where's the owner of this bar?"

He pointed with his arm and all of his fingers extended at the table halfway back where two men were sitting. As Liz walked back to the table, she popped a stick of chewing gum into her mouth and started chewing it.

When she got back to the table where the owner sat she said, "Hi."

"Hi there, darling," he said. "The job of the waitress has been filled."

"I'm not looking for a waitress job," she returned.

"Well, what can I do for you?"

"I am the lead singer in a local band, and I am looking to play a gig here, actually regular gigs."

"Really, what kind of music do you play? I hope not classical."

"Well, actually, we could handle that, too, but we get a much better response from rock-and-roll."

"Okay, well, that's great. We are booked for the rest of the month, but we can set something up for next month."

"Do you know Eli Animas?"

"I do know Eli. Why do you ask? Do you know him?"

"Yes, he is a friend of mine. Does he work here?"

"No, he used to work here. But then he fractured someone's nose and then they sued Eli and me for a lot of money. I don't think he paid a dime."

Liz wondered if Eli was financially stable but that proved to her that he was running from something. Now she had all the proof she needed. She was still intimidated to leave him, but decided that she and Roscoe would have to start planning the big getaway. The problem was that she had inherited the house from her mom, and she didn't want to have people there that she didn't like.

"So we need to fill out the contract if you are going to work at this bar. And I also need the signatures of all the people in the band."

Liz was silently but secretly doubting that that would happen.

"Okay," she said.

The paperwork took about twenty minutes, and then Liz took a moment to look at the small stage and quietly visualized were all the equipment would go. Then she thanked the owner and walked out of this bar.

As she was leaving the bar someone said, "Hi, baby."

That was followed by scattered laughter. She froze for a second, thinking that maybe she had missed Eli sitting there, and chills ran up her spine because she had just talked about him. She quickly looked back and saw a drunk lecherous man with stains on his shirt glaring at her. It was definitely not Eli, but she instantly pictured Eli at another bar, sucking on a shot glass. After she got over her shock, she quickly walked out into the sunlight. Her eyes fully dilated. As the pupils began to reduce, she closed them first. She slowly began to see again. Then she had a private celebration that she closed her first deal.

Even though she had wanted to walk away from that bar owner, she decided that her and Roscoe needed this gig more than her pride, and she bit her lip and walked out of the bar. For a moment, she wondered if she wanted to lower herself to get this job. But John had said that this would be good for Roscoe, so she decided she would give this a try, and if this didn't work out, they would just walk away. As she walked back to her car, the tears flowed freely. This is the environment that Eli was perfectly comfortable in and made her skin crawl.

When she got back to the house, Roscoe was counting the numbers on bios his watch. His eyes lit up when Liz walked through the door.

"Mom!" he said.

She just stood there shaking her head.

"Do you know where Eli is?" she said. She walked around the house saying his name, but Eli didn't answer. She began to realize that Roscoe had been left alone. She decided at that moment that she no longer needed or wanted Eli in her life anymore. She had decided this many times before but always withered when she faced her aggressive boyfriend.

Just then, she heard the door opening. She whipped around to see Eli walking in with a couple bags of groceries. She melted into a puddle of humiliation because she thought he had just dumped Roscoe to go drinking.

"What's up?" Eli said.

"Well, a moment ago, I was pissed because I thought you had left Roscoe here to go drinking or something."

"Just got some groceries."

"I see that, so I am sorry for not trusting you, but you can't leave him here alone."

"But I didn't think I could take care of him," Eli said as he gritted his teeth in his anger. He walked over to Liz and put his arms around her and clasped his hands together behind her back with his fists closed. And then started to squeeze her rib cage from behind.

"Eli, you are hurting me," she said as she tried to catch her breath.

THE GATE WAS OPEN

Eli looked at Roscoe who was shaking his head and was mouthing, "No."

"Yeah, what are you going to do about it, old man?"

"Eli, leave him alone," she said, trying to recover.

"I have to put the groceries away now," he said.

"No, Eli. I think it would be best if you moved out."

"What the hell are you talking about Liz? You need me!"

"Actually, now that we got a gig we are going to be busy, and I think we need to go our separate ways," she said with a small, shy frown.

He walked over to her and held his fist right in front of her face. She stayed calm but wondered if she was about to die.

"Look, I don't want to fight with you, but let's talk about this. You get rid of me and you will be sorry."

"Hmm," she said.

"Which bar did you get a gig in?" he said as he put the milk in the refrigerator.

"Jack's Juke Joint," Liz said.

"I used to work there."

"Yeah. They hate you because you caused a lawsuit there."

"It was self-defense!"

"You know with you, Eli, it's always self-defense!" she said as she looked at Roscoe who was standing in the corner, hiding his face. She walked over to him and gently rubbed her hand on his back.

"Roscoe, do you want to go to the mall to practice?"

The frown turned into a smile and he was nodding. Then Liz looked out the living room window and saw the gate was open.

"Eli, the gate is open, and there's a dog who enjoys relieving itself in my yard."

"Right now?"

"No. It's the mysterious dog, and I have never seen it, but I have to dodge the land mines even in the middle of the sidewalk."

"Well, I didn't leave it open. Maybe Roscoe did."

"You see? That's what I'm talking about. If you are leaving the gate open, who knows where he might go?"

"Well, look, I'm not a wet nurse, and I can't baby sit him all the time. There must be places in town that can do that."

"The one place in this town that takes seniors is full."

"Well, I don't have a crystal ball, so I don't know what to do with him."

"John is going to help me figure out how to get Medicare for him, and SSI to help take care of him. I checked at the bank and they will not release his money to anyone but him and I don't even know how much money he has. Or how to even do a withdraw of his money. I was told I would need to apply to become a POA."

"A POA or a DOA?"

"Why do you always think of death?"

"I don't. He did the symbol of the gun the first time."

"Well, you seem to constantly belabor the subject."

"By the way, Liz, I walked down to the basement today, and way back in the corner over there, I found two bags of clothes. They are men's clothes, so I brought them up here. Maybe Roscoe could wear them."

"Where did you put them?"

Eli pointed at two grocery bags sitting against the wall.

"Did you want me to ask at work tonight if you could play at the bar I work at?"

"The more the merrier."

It was dark out, and Eli got his stuff together to go into work. After he left, Liz walked over to the two bags of clothes and looked through them. As she picked up a pair of khaki pants, she felt a hard object in the pants pocket. She reached into the pocket and withdrew a two-by-two inch fabric pouch that had been hand-sewn on all four sides, and she could feel something hard inside.

She carried the pouch into the kitchen, and with a steak knife, she cut the stitching around the two-inch piece of fabric. As she was doing that, a ring dropped out of the pouch and bounced on the floor. She looked down into the glinting surfaces of the diamond. The first thing that went through her mind was, *I'm glad Eli isn't home now.*

She bent down and picked it up and stared at the glistening stone. *Wow, that must have cost a fortune.*

As Liz continued to study the ring, she saw words on the inside of the gold band: "To…My… Love… Becky."

"Oh my god," Liz actually verbalized this time. Her mind started to spin out of control.

I thought they had only been together only for a one-night stand. How did my mother get all those clothes that were obviously Roscoe's?

So many questions coursed through her mind. *How could this be?* she pondered.

They must have spent more time together then my mother was willing to share with me. Where did all these clothes come from that were left in the basement for decades? Why didn't he give her the ring? she wondered.

She looked up at a picture of her mother and a picture of herself, and they looked like twins. Then Liz slipped the ring on her finger, it was a little tight, but she managed to get it on.

She walked over to Roscoe and said, "Roscoe, where did you get this ring?"

He merrily gazed down at the ring and smiled a toothy grin. "It's for you, Mom."

She shook her head again which had become a frequent response to everything that amazed her.

"Well, thanks, Roscoe. That is so kind of you. And I accept this in my mother's absence."

Then she tried to take the ring off and realized it was stuck and a cold sweat broke out on her face.

What was she going to do if Eli saw this?

CHAPTER 26

2005

Liz went to another bar to set up another date where she and Roscoe could play. In the meantime, she kept the hand with the ring on it in her pocket. She had tried to wiggle it off. Then she had tried to use some mineral oil to lubricate the finger and allow in to slide off. But one of her knuckles hurt too much, and as she worked with the ring, the knuckle started to swell. That was the major roadblock, and no matter what she tried, the knuckle wouldn't release. She felt the heat building up in her face because she couldn't leave this ring on. She thought about her ribs which still were very painful, and Liz was afraid that he had cracked one of them.

Meanwhile, the anger was building up in Eli. How could she kick him out of the house? She doesn't pay anything to live here. He was helping her take care of the old man, and he had always helped her out. He protected her from the last creep she was dating. Eli knew all the bars in this small town, and after Liz had left, he locked the doors to make sure that Roscoe wouldn't run away. Then he crawled through one of the windows and got into his car and started off visiting each bar in the town. At the third bar, he saw her car and then he parked and walked into the bar. She was talking to the to a person who he assumed was the bar owner or manager. She was laughing and chatting. So Eli sat down at an empty stool at the bar.

"What ya havin', buddy?" the bartender said. She was an older woman that looked like she had been run through the wringer.

"Whatever you got that will help me forget my girlfriend," he said, glancing back at Liz.

"Well, that's a pretty wide range. I could give you something that would help you forget everything that was ever in your mind."

"That will do."

"So you want some rot gut?"

"Yeah or rubbing alcohol."

"Wow, you got it bad, my friend. Well, there is a drug store down the street."

"Give me a shot of whatever is in your hand," he said as he looked back at Liz. He stared at her and saw something flashing on her left hand as it picked up the spotlight from overhead. He felt a lot of anger rising up in his solar plexus.

What the hell is that, did she run off and marry someone else?

Then he decided to get out of that bar because he wanted to confront her at the house. He stood up and walked out of the bar without being seen. Because he had the goods on her and he wanted to catch her in the act.

He drove back to the house at a high rate of speed. When he walked in, Roscoe was counting the numbers on his watch again. Then he flopped down on the couch in a position that he could see the front door. He lay there with his eyes barely open. When Liz got home, after the door swung open she quickly slid her hand into her pocket. He clearly saw the huge diamond on her finger in the half second it was exposed. She was obviously happy.

"What are you so happy about?" he said.

"Oh, I just got us another gig."

"Yeah, and that's not the only thing you got."

"What are you talking about?" she said punching her hand down into her pocket.

"You know damn well what I am talking about. Who gave you that ring?"

"The what?"

He bolted up off the couch and grabbed her arm and yanked it out of her pocket. And there was the two carat diamond.

"What is this?" he said, grabbing her wrist.

"Shit, why do you enjoy hurting me so much?"

Roscoe was over in his corner quivering.

"I want to know what the hell you are up to."

"You are drunk."

"I am looking at a huge diamond ring, and I wish I was drunk," he said. "Did you pull a fast one on me and marry someone else?"

She pushed him away, and then he reached out and smacked her across her face. Roscoe was frozen in fear.

"It's not what you think. I found this in one of Roscoe's pockets."

"That's bullshit. What would Roscoe be doing with a diamond ring? The guy can't even comb his hair." Then he shouted, "Hey, Roscoe, did you have a ring for Liz… I mean for Mom?"

"Ahh…"

"Yeah, so someone is lying here, and there could only be one person that knows how to lie."

"If I could get this ring off my finger, you would see it is inscribed with 'To my love, Becky.' That would be my mother and the ring belongs to my father," she said, pointing to Roscoe.

"Well, take it off," he said.

"It's not my ring, so it's stuck on my finger!"

"Well, why did you put it on your finger?"

"It was beautiful, and it is part of my parent's history."

"You better not be lying to me!"

"And what are you going to do if I am?"

"Don't push me, Liz," Eli barked out as he looked at Roscoe who was glaring at him.

"Roscoe, let's get out of here!"

Roscoe squatted down and vomited on the floor.

"Oh shit. Now you see what you did," she said and then got Roscoe cleaned up and into bed.

"I'm going to the jewelry store to get this ring cut off and find out how much it's worth. You take care of Roscoe. He is too sick to travel."

"And you know whatever it's worth, it's mine," Eli said.

"What the hell are you talking about?"

"I found the clothes in the basement, and obviously, that's where it was."

"But they weren't your clothes. They are Roscoe's clothes, and my mom's name is on the inside."

"Hey, finders keepers!"

"Get lost, you jerk," she said.

"You are cutting into my rest time."

"Well, can I trust you to take care of Roscoe while I take care of this situation?"

"Yeah, whatever."

Liz left the house and drove to the mall. she knew there was a jewelry store in there. Eli flopped down on the couch, but he couldn't turn his mind off.

I need to take care of this problem.

He walked to the bedroom and took his Glock 9mm out of the drawer where he had stashed it. Then he came back into the living room and set the Glock on the coffee table.

Roscoe walked out of the bedroom and looked at Eli. "Where's Mom? I need to use the bathroom."

"Come here a second, Roscoe."

"But I need to use the bathroom," Roscoe said as he walked over to Eli.

"Remember, when we talked about Liz—ah, no, I mean Mom. Remember when we talked about what you would do if mom left you?"

Roscoe shook his head from side to side with a look of trepidation on his face.

"No, of course you don't remember that. Well, let me refresh your memory a little bit." Eli made his hand into the shape of a gun and put the tip of his index finger on his temple.

"Do you remember this?" Eli asked.

Roscoe nodded his head slightly and had a frown on his face.

"Well, guess what?" Eli said.

"What?" Roscoe responded.

"Liz is gone. She left us! She left us!" Eli said with his arms out and his palms up as if to indicate that he didn't know.

"No!" Roscoe said.

"Yup, she's gone," Eli responded.

"Mom, no!"

"So what are we going to do?" Eli said.

"Mom's gone?"

"That's right. She's gone forever."

Roscoe just sat there shaking his head from side to side, and his frown became more pronounced as Eli sat his Glock 9mm on the table in front of Roscoe.

"Well, I am sorry, Roscoe, but I am so sad about this, and I think I am going to leave too."

Roscoe looked very sad as he processed this information. Eli cocked the gun and handed it to him. Roscoe held the gun in his hand and looked at it. Eli was pretending he was sad and had his hand over his eyes. Roscoe lifted the gun up and put the barrel against his temple. Eli peeked out through a couple of his fingers. He covered his face to prevent any blowback of blood or gray matter. He slid his chair back to get further away from the mess. He had the perfect excuse, and he had a change of clothes all ready in case he got anything on his clothes. Roscoe took the gun and moved it away from his head.

"We got to do this, Roscoe. We are alone and so sad."

Roscoe moved the gun back to his head in one movement. Eli covered his face again expecting the boom.

Nothing.

He looked at Roscoe, the gun was in place, his finger was on the trigger and tears were streaming down his face. Roscoe's mind was spinning out of control as he tried so hard to process this information. He actually remembered the last year and the difficulties Liz had with Eli. He remembered the joy he felt while he and Liz were playing music. And so wished they could play again, but someone was telling him it would never happen again.

Eli was getting frustrated again, and he put his hands over his face again. Then in another quick and decisive move, Roscoe leveled the gun on Eli's head and pulled the trigger. The air was heavy with the smell of gunpowder. And there was a white haze in the air. Roscoe felt the blood droplets hitting his face, and the pain of the gun hitting him. If he had been conscious at this point, his ears would be ringing. Eli was thrown back and blood and gray matter were thrown all over the wall behind him. The body dropped straight down to the floor.

A puddle of blood was forming under Eli's head. When Roscoe pulled the trigger, the gun kicked back, freeing itself from Roscoe's hand, and it hit him in his left eye. He collapsed on the floor, unconscious. And the Glock slid across the floor. The back of Eli's head had been blown completely off. He had died before he hit the floor.

* * *

Liz walked into the jewelry store.

"Hello, ma'am."

"Hi. Listen, I put my mom's ring on and it got stuck on my finger."

"Yeah, that happens a lot."

"Do you know how to get this off?"

"Sure, but we will have to cut the ring. But you will still have your finger."

"Yeah, I figured as much,"

The jewelry clerk slid a small jaw from a pair of pliers under the ring. He closed the pliers and the toothed wheel came down the ring. He turned a thumb screw, and the toothed wheel started cutting the ring. Soon, the ring was cut through, and then Liz was able to pull it off because the ring was free to expand.

CHAPTER 27

2005

When the door opened, she could sense something was amiss. There were no voices, no noise at all except for a bird chirping in the yard. With the door open, she could see a slight haze of white smoke and the breeze coming in the front door caused it to swirl. There was also the odor of burnt gunpowder that hung in the air. She was afraid to enter, but something told her that she had to move into what she knew was hell.

As she got a couple inches past the door frame, she caught the first glimpse of trouble. Eli was lying supine and his eyes were open, but there was something wrong with this picture. And that was the third eye, or was it an eye? She grabbed onto the door frame with a steel grip and the splinter that punctured her skin was not felt in anyway. As she looked at Eli, it appeared that his head was sunken into the floor or actually that it was sunken a dark red puddle. She immediately felt a hot liquid rising up her esophagus, and instantly, it was in her mouth. She could have swallowed it, but the taste was much like putting the terminals of a battery on her tongue. She opted to spit the fluid out and with it, the acidic taste. The fluid splashed on the floor, and then she shook her head to clear the dizziness out and get control of herself.

What was she seeing? How could this be? She averted her eyes to a different direction to relieve her anxiety. And then she saw Roscoe also lying face up on the floor behind the couch. He was facing the ceiling, but his eyes were closed. There was a dark area around his left eye. She wanted to run away from this nightmare that no one would want to gaze upon. She walked gingerly over to Roscoe as if she was sneaking up on him and bent over to look at his face. There was a very dark bruise around his left eye. Then she saw Eli's gun sitting on the floor. Liz quickly looked for a gunshot wound or blood or anything that would indicate a fatal wound. She got down on her knees and bent down to look at his eye. She could hear breathing and could see the rise and fall of his ribcage. Liz put her hand on his forehead to feel for warmth.

Roscoe's right eye flew open.

"Ahhhh…" she screamed and fell backward on to her back. His left eye couldn't open because it was swollen shut. As Liz looked at Roscoe's eye after she regained her composure, she could almost see the bruise expanding.

"Mom?" he said.

"Roscoe, what happened here?" she said almost screaming.

All Roscoe did was point at the ceiling. Liz quickly ran to the phone and dialed 911.

"Where's your emergency?"

"In my house."

"What's your address, ma'am?"

"136 Rosebud," Liz responded.

"What's your emergency?"

"I don't know what happened. My boyfriend is dead, and I think my dad is hurt real bad."

"Are both people breathing?"

"Nooo!" My boyfriend's head is almost missing. And my dad looks like he got into a fight with a prize fighter."

"Law enforcement and EMS have been dispatched, and they will be there shortly. Is there anyone else in the house?"

"Ah, I don't think so."

That's when Liz looked at the Glock pistol sitting on the floor about three feet away from Roscoe.

My god, what the hell happened here? she thought. She looked up at the ceiling and saw nothing.

"Roscoe, what happened here?"

Roscoe put his hands together, palms touching, fingers pointing skyward, and said, "The gate was open."

"What gate?"

He raised one hand up toward the ceiling.

"I was protecting you, Mom!"

Oh shit, he didn't do what I think he did.

"Roscoe, don't say anything else about this to anyone."

"Okay, Mom."

"Are you hurt?"

"This hurts," he said, pointing to his eye.

Liz heard the sirens as all disciplines of emergency services converged on the house. The first people were law enforcement and the other services were told to stage at a safe distance. Two police officers approached the house with guns drawn. The front door was still open since Liz was so shocked by the scene she forgot all the normal things people do when they walk into their house. The first officer approached her front door from the side. The other officer covered from a short distance. When the first officer looked around the corner into the living room of the house, he started yelling orders.

"Hands up!"

"Okay," Liz muttered. When you were standing there with your hands up you often feel like you were naked. Especially when you are totally innocent.

"Lie face down on the floor and don't move."

Both officers swung into the living room. Facing different directions.

"Clear right."

"Clear left."

The second officer went over to Liz and put hand cuffs around her wrists.

"But I didn't do anything!" she said.

The officers continued through the house, stopping to handcuff Roscoe, and then they hit every room and closet in the house, saying, "Clear," with every room. As yet no one had spoken to Liz.

When they had the house cleared, each officer went to one of the people in the house. The officer that went to Roscoe said, "Gun,"

THE GATE WAS OPEN

and picked up the Glock cleared the chamber and removed the clip. Then he checked Roscoe's wrist.

"I got a pulse on this one!"

"No pulse over here," the other officer said. But he knew that was going to be the case after observing the scene.

"Mom."

"It's okay, Roscoe. I'll explain everything."

"Officer, Roscoe has dementia and doesn't have much cognitive functioning."

Still no response from the police officers. Then one of the officers started speaking into his radio.

"House is clear, need EMS in the house."

At that point, the front door became a revolving door. The paramedics came in with their bags and electronic equipment. They took one look at Eli, checked for pulses, and then covered the body with a sheet. They focused on Roscoe next, and since he was alive, they started asking questions. Roscoe was in handcuffs at this point too.

"Sir, do you have any pain?"

"Mom!"

"I'm going to examine you now. Let me know if you have any pain."

"I want Mom!"

The medics looked at each other and one said, "Mentally challenged." The other one nodded.

After that, the detectives walked in and they handcuffed Liz and helped the medics load Roscoe on to a stretcher and one of them accompanied the ambulance to the hospital. The other detective stayed at the house and photographed as much of the scene as possible. Then the coroner showed up and also took pictures of the body, but the detectives were not ready to release the body, so Eli stayed right where he fell. They also used a laser to get the trajectory of the bullet from the hole it left in the wall behind the point where Eli's body was. Doing that would help them estimate the height of the gun when the fatal shot occurred. And that would let them extrapolate the shooter's height. One of the detectives reached into Eli's back pocket and removed a wallet. He jotted some notes down and them handed the wallet to the coroner.

A few neighbors lingered on the sidewalk in front of the house, and the press showed up because a murder was big news in a small town. But no one was calling it a murder at this time. The detectives interviewed the neighbors and found out that the couple that lived in 136 Rosebud were often heard yelling at each other. The curiosity of the other man in the house made things more complicated. Especially since they couldn't get any information from him. Liz was taken to the police station, and Roscoe went with the ambulance to the emergency department.

"So, Liz, is it okay that I call you that?"

"Well, that's my name," she said.

"Okay, so tell me what happened at 136 Rosebud today."

"I don't know. I wasn't there."

"Well, you live there, don't you?"

"Of course, I live there!"

"And who else lives there?"

"My father and my boyfriend. Well, I think I can say, 'used to live there' because obviously Eli isn't living anywhere now."

"And that is Roscoe Gillette and Eli Animas?"

"Yes, of course," she replied.

Victims who are affected by crime are often put off by questions that law enforcement ask because it becomes somewhat obvious that they are trying to catch people in mistakes or trying to evaluate whether they are lying. Meanwhile, the victims are caught off guard because they were going throughout their everyday life, and suddenly, a bomb is dropped in their lap and oftentimes people can't remember things that they do every day. That was exactly the situation with Liz. She was totally taken off guard at first, but as the questioning continued, she began to think that she was the target and she began to guard her answers.

Meanwhile, the detective in the ambulance let the medics do what they had to do, but he listened very carefully to any answer that Roscoe provided. These answers were few and far between because Roscoe was threatened by this situation and simply stared at the person asking the question. The medics were forced to rely on signs and not so much on symptoms. The most obvious sign was his face with the dramatic purple bruise and a small laceration above the eye.

When they got to the emergency department at the local hospital, the detective took two cotton swabs out of his pocket and collected two drops of blood from Roscoe's face and put them in the tubes that kept them from getting contaminated. He slid the tubes back into his pocket and then stepped aside when the nurses and doctor came into the room to examine him.

Roscoe looked at the detective and said, "I want Mom."

"Yeah, you and me both dude."

The doctor ordered facial X-rays all over Roscoe's face. He was especially interested in the frontal sinus and other bones around Roscoe's left orbit. When Roscoe went to X-ray, the doctor came over to the detective and asked a few questions.

"Detective, do you know what happened to him?"

"No, but we found him at the scene of a murder, and he has not provided much information but he seems to have a problem with his brain. I don't know, doc. I thought you were going to tell me what was going on with him."

"Okay, we will do the standard tests, and that will probably disclose something."

"Yeah, but he is not very talkative, and I don't know if he is hiding something or if this is a medical problem."

In the meantime, Liz was taken to the police station and booked in. The police had to cover every possibility that might be significant. At the same time, Matthew Samms walked into the room. Garland was the lead detective for the department and had decided to throw everything into this because murders were pretty rare. He got all the information from the other detective and sent him home because his shift was about to end. Since this witness wasn't all that talkative, he assigned a uniformed officer to monitor him and then he went back to the station to interview the one that could give some information.

"Hi, Miss Gillette,"

Liz just looked at the new detective that walked into the interview room.

"Can you take these handcuffs off?"

"It's just procedure, ma'am."

"You really treat innocent people like this?"

"Nobody is innocent until we prove them innocent."

"I think you have that backward. Innocent until proven guilty."

"Whatever you say," Garland said as he unlocked the cuffs.

"I wasn't even at the scene of this crime."

"Actually, you were right in the middle of the crime scene when we entered."

"But I wasn't at the scene when the crime occurred."

"Yeah, everyone says that. So where were you when this went down?"

"I had to go to a jewelry store," Liz said.

"Had to go?"

"Yeah, I had to get this ring cut off."

"That's interesting. Why did you have to get a ring cut off?"

"Because it wasn't mine and once it was on, I couldn't get it off," Liz replied as she set the ring on the table.

Matt picked the ring up and dropped it into a plastic bag. "Okay," he said.

"What are you doing?"

"Evidence. It could save your life."

"What?"

"Who's ring was it?"

"My mother's, and it is pretty special to me," Liz said.

"Wow, this gets more interesting every minute."

"Don't get too excited."

"Where is your mother now?"

"Six feet under."

"How did she die?"

"Ovarian cancer."

"My condolences," Garland said.

"She died twenty-five years ago."

"And you've been wearing a ring for twenty-five years that could threaten your finger?"

"No, just a couple days."

"Where did you get the ring?"

"From my dad, and that's why it is so special to me, so you better not lose it."

"That's a pretty big ring. I guess your dad was doing pretty good."

"What did you do with him?" Liz asked.

"He's fine. Being taken care of. Why don't you fill in the gaps Liz."

"What do you mean by that?"

"You know damn well what I mean. Who killed Eli?"

"I dropped into the middle of this mess when I opened the door of my house. And I think the options are pretty small."

"Did you and Eli ever fight?"

"Do you and your wife ever fight?" Liz retorted.

"I'll ask the questions and you answer them, or we will never get anywhere, Liz."

"Yes, Eli and I fought all the time."

"What did you fight about?"

"You know, Eli is one of those controlling types, and he was pissed that I moved my dad into the house. He had to take his punching bag down. Actually, I cut it down. It was his pride and joy."

"Were you defending yourself?"

"Look, I can see that you aren't trying to trap me in a corner."

"Just trying to get the facts."

"By the way, my dad has dementia and I need to take care of him. When can I see him?"

"He's in good hands… Do you think your dad could have killed Eli?"

"A couple days ago, Eli told me that Roscoe couldn't even comb his hair, so to think that he could figure out how to use a gun is very doubtful."

"Who's gun was it?"

"That was Eli's."

"Do you know how you use it?"

"You just won't give up, do you?"

"If I gave up, I wouldn't be serving the town that I was sworn to protect."

"I hate firearms, and I don't own one so it's doubtful that I could use that gun."

"One more question, Liz."

"Promise?"

"Why does Roscoe call you Mom?"

CHAPTER 28

2005

Liz got her one call.

The phone in John's office rang.

"Hello?" he said.

"John?"

"Yes?"

"John, this is Liz Gillette. I need your help."

"What's up, Liz?"

"Roscoe is in the ER and I am unable to be with him. Since you were the one person he connected with and you understand him so well, would you be willing to go to the ER to make sure he is doing okay?"

"Ah, yeah, I guess. Where are you?"

"I'm in…jail."

"*What?*" The thoughts that ran through John's head were wild.

"That's right, but Roscoe has no one that knows him, to take care of him."

"Well, Liz you need to fill in the blanks here. Why is Roscoe in the ER and why are you in jail?"

Liz paused for a moment. "In time, I can explain everything to you."

"Where is Eli?"

"Eli is dead."

John had to cover up a slight smile. "Okay, no more discussion on this matter. I will go to the ER to check on Roscoe."

"Thanks," she said.

John's office and the ER were in the same building. He took the elevator down to the ground floor. When he got to the emergency department, he walked up to the ground floor. When he got to the emergency department, he walked up to the charge nurse. He pulled an identification card out of his pocket and then introduced himself.

"I'm John Mckenize with Adult Protective Services."

"Hi, John. What can I do for you?"

"I'm here to see Roscoe Gillette."

"Good. Maybe you can get some information out of him, I think the detective may have taken his tongue."

John's head quickly swung back with a slight snort. "Well, where is he?"

"He is just back from CAT scan and now he is in room five."

"Thanks," John said. John walked into the room and nodded to the detective.

"I am John McKenzie, and I am with Adult Protective Services, and I have evaluated Mr. Gillette." He shook the detective's hand.

"Hi, John. So do you speak his language?"

"I am sorry. His language is English. Oh, I understand." John laughed out loud. "Yeah, he's been confusing people with what comes out of his mouth for a long time."

John knew why Roscoe was saying, "Where's Mom?" but he was uncertain of Liz's status, so he choose to keep as much information as he could to himself. The detective was observing John and Roscoe to see if he could pick up any clues.

"Hi, Roscoe," John said.

Roscoe recognized John and had a vague memory of him being friendly with Liz and also that they had had some good conversations.

"Hi," Roscoe said tentatively.

John was talking to Roscoe when he saw the man's eyes immediately go to the door. John looked at the door and standing in the doorway was Matthew Samms. He gave the other detective a signal with his fingers to indicate he wanted to talk in private. The two men walked out to the hallway. John changed his attention back to Roscoe.

"How are you doing, Roscoe?"

Roscoe smiled and said, "Where's Mom?"

John grinned and said, "I knew you were going to go there. Listen, Liz wanted me to come see how you were doing. Are they taking care of you?"

Roscoe just nodded and pointed to his eye. "This hurts."

"Yeah. It will probably hurt for a while, but it will get better."

John knew better than to ask Roscoe for any details, especially with the two detectives right outside the door. Then a surprising thing happened. As John looked at Roscoe, the elderly man winked at him. It got John thinking that Roscoe had something to say. John made a mental note to take this up with Roscoe and Liz at a later time. The detectives walked back into the room.

"So you are with Adult Protective Services?" Matt said with a questioning inflection.

"Yes, sir," John said.

"Are you an attorney?"

"No, I work for the hospital," John said.

"And we are responsible for taking this man into custody," Matt said.

"No, you can't take him anywhere."

"Say that again," Matt responded.

"I'm sorry, detective, but you are on hospital property, and this man is mentally incapacitated. I work for Adult Protective Services, and it is my responsibility to represent him while he is in the hospital."

Roscoe was watching both men as they sparred and his eyes looked like a couple of Ping-Pong balls as each man spoke.

"So you don't have any legal experience?"

"No, sir, but you have his power of attorney in jail, so I have to step up to represent him, and I am in the position of his temporary POA."

Matt walked to the other detective and whispered in his ear. The second detective nodded and walked out of the room. At the same time, the doctor walked back into the room.

"Gentlemen, you will have to take your meeting into the hallway."

Then a nurse came in with a metal tray wrapped in blue sterilization wrapping. Inside the wrapping were tools needed for suturing a laceration. The doctor first injected Roscoe's wound with a lidocaine, then he started sewing the laceration.

"Where's Mom?" Roscoe asked.

"I'm sorry, sir. I don't know where your mom is," the doctor said as he glanced at John and Garland with a smile on his face.

As they got into the hallway, the conversation continued.

"You see, detective, that man is lost in some other universe. He can use his legs, he can use his arms, but his mind is gone."

"Possibly, but you have to be in this universe to pull a trigger."

"That's true," John said. "But Roscoe would not survive in prison."

"And the fact that prison would be hard on him does not mean he cannot go there."

"I understand that, detective, but what if a child picked up a gun and killed his parent, would you sentence that child to life in prison or would you give that child a chance to rehabilitate?"

"Guess what, John, that's not a decision for me. That's up to a judge to decide."

"That's also true, but it just tears my heart out to throw this guy in a cell. He needs his daughter to take care of him."

"You know we can't have a lawless society where people just go around blowing over people away."

"But I got the feeling that Mr. Animas was very hard on both Liz and Roscoe."

"I understand, but you are basically just being a judge and jury. You have to let the legal process run its course."

"Well, I think that we will put him in a memory care facility. They are all lockdown units, so the residents can't wander off."

"Yeah, just make sure he doesn't have any contact with any knives or anything."

"Your right...then Liz can come and visit him."

"But we are getting ahead of yourselves. We haven't done our investigation yet. This could be other players in this picture, including Liz or even you, John."

"You don't know Liz, detective."

"Do you, sir? You seem to think you know how criminal minds work. I've seen many things that I would have never thought of until we completed the investigation."

"Okay, Detective Morris. I will let you do your job and just see where the chips fall."

"Thank you, sir."

"Is it okay if I go to the station and give Liz a report that Roscoe is being taken care of."

"You are free to do whatever you would like, but Miss Gillette is in custody because she is also a possible suspect."

"So what you are saying is that both of these people need an attorney."

John arrived at the police station about ten minutes later.

"Excuse me, ma'am," he said to the receptionist.

"Yes?"

"I am here to see a friend of mine who is being detained."

"Name, please."

"Liz Gillette."

"Okay, you need to talk to the captain at the desk over there."

"Thank you."

John walked over to the burly-looking police captain at the front desk. When he got to the captain, he could smell aftershave coming from him.

"Hello, sir."

"What can I do for you."

"A friend of mine is being detained here and I came to talk to her."

"Your name?"

"John McKenzie for Liz Gillette."

"Okay. Give me a second, and I will move her to an interview room."

"Thank you, Captain."

A few minutes later, John was moved to an interview room.

"Hi, Liz."

"Hi, John," she said. "How is Roscoe doing?"

"First of all, let me apologize for leaving him, but he's not far from here, only about ten minutes."

"Who's watching him?"

"There is a pretty hard-driving detective trying to extract as much information from him as he can."

"How's Roscoe holding up?"

"He is the same, constantly asking for mom. And a doctor was sewing up his laceration when I left."

"I need to get back to him."

"Well, it's not up to me," John said.

"I don't know what happened to Eli."

John didn't say anything, he just shook his head and put his fingers to his lips. John pointed up at the smoke detector on the ceiling and Liz glanced up and then started nodding. Liz closed her eyes and sighed a little and started talking about the weather. After about ten minutes, a detective walked into the interview room.

"What are you planning, dude?"

"I was talking to Liz about her father who I am very concerned about."

"Why are you so concerned about Mr. Gillette?"

"Because his cognitive abilities are very limited."

"Who pulled the trigger at her house?" he said, pointing at Liz with a very aggressive tone to his voice.

Liz and John had blank looks on their faces. Then John spoke. "Sir, Roscoe Gillette has a very serious problem with his cognitive processes."

"So are you saying he pulled the trigger?"

"I don't know who killed Eli Animas. Maybe it was someone you aren't even thinking of."

"And who would that be? Are you putting yourself in the running?"

"Please investigate me," John said. "I was working all day, and I was around other people in the hospital."

"We will look into that."

"Yes, sir, and I welcome that," John said.

The detective left the room, and John and Liz looked at each other.

"I am going to contact a public defender for you and Roscoe. I have go, and my biggest concern is Roscoe, so I will spend most of my time with him."

"Okay. I appreciate that John."

John left the police station and returned to the hospital.

CHAPTER 29

2005

"Really?"

"Yes, sir."

"What do you mean you didn't do GSR tests on the suspects!"

"I didn't have any paper bags in my car."

"Damn, you could have tossed this whole case! When their attorney gets a hold of this, we are sunk."

"Yes, sir."

"Well, I'll swab him now," Matt said.

"If you say so."

"The guy from Adult Protective Services is at the cop shop so let's keep this between ourselves, you got that?"

"Yes, sir."

Matt Samms took two cotton swabs and put them in his shirt pocket. When he walked back into the hospital room, the doctor had just finished suturing Roscoe's forehead and now had a Frankenstein look to him. Matt waited till doctor exited the room and casually walked over to the bed and glanced down at the suture tray now sitting on a metal tray beside the bed. The ER was having a busy day, and people were in and out of the room quickly. Matt walked over to Roscoe.

"Hi, Roscoe," Matt said.

Matt lifted Roscoe's left hand and quickly swabbed his palm and between his fingers and then slid the swab into a clear plastic tube. Once the first hand was done, he set it down and lifted the right hand. This was probably the key hand, and he started swabbing it.

"It just never ends!" the nurse said as she walked back into the ER room, to clean up the suture tray.

Matt quickly dropped Roscoe's hand and tucked the swab down by his leg. "Yeah, I'm afraid you are right," Matt said.

"Where does he go after this?"

"Well, I will probably take him back to the police station where his daughter is."

"Man, I thought I had a tough job, but you guys have to deal with all this crime."

"You get used to it," Matt said, trying to be friendly.

"Did I miss a cotton swab?"

"Ah…no, I don't think so."

"Oh, I thought I saw one in your hand."

Matt lifted the hand without the swab in it. "Nope, nothing up my sleeve." He started blushing hard.

"Okay, I just have to be sure. You know the HIPAA rules really keep you hopping."

The nurse bent down to pick up something up off the floor, and that's when she saw the cotton swab in his right hand by his leg.

"Do you want me to take that swab?"

"No I was just…scratching my ear."

The nurse looked at him askew.

"Okay, whatever. Just can't leave the room dirty."

"No, you did a great job."

She walked out, and he quickly swabbed Roscoe's other hand and stowed the swab in its protective case.

At the crime lab, the forensic technician gloved up and removed the Glock 9mm out of the plastic bag and gingerly set it on the table. He knew that getting a good print was very difficult if not impossible on a gun. The reasons for that were many, people don't always touch a gun in a way that will leave a good print on many guns. Many have offset or serrated surfaces so that a person can maintain a good grip on the weapon. Matt Samms had called and told them that a potential suspect had a laceration on his forehead, and they should focus on the hammer on the back of the gun. The technician first made sure the gun was safe.

He removed the magazine and made sure there was not a round in the chamber. The bullets in the magazine are the best place to find finger prints. Unfortunately, the deceased man had prints on every bullet in the magazine, and no other prints could be lifted. Several tiny flakes of dried blood fell down on the clean paper on the table in the forensics lab. The tech continued using a sterile scalpel to try and loosen as much blood evidence as he could.

Later in the day, Matt Samms returned to the police station. He knew the public defender would be there soon, and Liz would be released.

"Hi Liz," he said as he entered the cell.

"Detective! Funny meeting you here," Liz said.

"Really, how funny is it?"

"How long are you going to hold me in this place?"

"I'm not holding you!"

"So I can leave?"

"I'm surprised you are still here."

"That's bullshit!" Liz said. "If I would have walked out of here, you would have shot me down."

"No, ma'am. You are free to go," he said, knowing that if he had enough time, he could get into her head.

A large rotund man walked up to the pair.

"Oh, look at that," Matt said. "The public defender shows up just as you are looking for him, Liz."

Liz just sat there looking at the two men thinking that she was the butt of a cruel joke. "I'm too tired for this stupidity."

"Can we go detective?" the public defender asked.

"Yeah, I was just telling Liz that she was free to go. But Liz don't leave town, I may have more questions for you."

"I'm Josh Brahams," the public defender said.

"I'm Liz Gillette."

"Hello, Miss Gillette. I was called by John Morris. He said you may need a little help, and I will be your public defender."

"No, I don't need your help. I didn't do anything."

"Right. I understand that, but I am thinking you need a little protection from an overzealous police department."

"Yeah, you're right about that."

"Now, I was told your father is involved in this whole thing, too."

"Yes, he is."

"Where is your father?"

"We are going to find him right now in the hospital."

"Why is he in the hospital?"

"So you don't know the whole story of this event."

"John filled me in briefly. Why don't we talk while I drive you to the hospital," Josh said, and the shocks on the car sagged when he got in.

"Yes. He was injured in this whole mess."

"He wasn't injured by the police, was he?"

"No. So I came home to a nightmare. My boyfriend was dead with his head blown off, and my dad was unconscious in my house."

Josh had a digital recorder and was getting everything like all good attorneys do.

"And John told me your dad has some medical problems."

"Yeah, he has dementia, and I know how this looks, but I can assure you, my dad could not have done this."

"How can you be so sure?"

"He is like a three-year-old."

"Do you have anybody else in mind?"

"Eli is one of those guys that pisses everybody off, so there is a long list of candidates."

"Did Eli ever beat you up or was he abusive in any way?"

"No."

"Well, you just said he pisses everyone off, so what was your relationship like."

"Well… Actually, he has hit me, and he has done things to show me that he could hurt me."

"Why did you say no at first?"

"Because I know the police, and even my attorney, would automatically assume that I had a vendetta against him."

"Did you?"

"No! But I was thinking of leaving him because now I have my hands full with my dad, and Eli was very eager to get his hands on my dad's money."

"How much money are we talking?"

"Hard to say."

"And look, Liz, I am your attorney so you can say anything to me and it won't end up in court. And I know it seems like I am being hard on you, but I am just preparing you for what the prosecutor will do."

"Okay, well, I didn't know how that worked."

"I am your advocate. I have your back and it is my job to keep you out of jail and living a free life."

Liz started weeping as the amazing weight of this day and the preceding months taking care of Roscoe all came down to one amazing eruption of tears. The water works were virtually non-ending, and she couldn't talk for at least ten minutes. Josh was used to these pent up emotional releases, so he sat down to let her cry it out.

"From now on, Liz, you will not talk to the police unless I am there."

"Really?"

"Really!"

"But they pressure you to a point that you say things you don't want to say, just to get them off your back."

"You can't let your guard down. Just say, 'No comment,' or you want your attorney present."

"You know the other thing, Josh, Roscoe and I were on the verge of starting a band and that would have been great for Roscoe because he relives his youth. And that is a very important thing because when you have dementia, memories are precious."

"Well, you can keep playing because they can't put you in jail until there is a verdict."

Then they pulled into the ER parking lot. Liz and Josh walked into the emergency department entryway.

"You know what they say, Liz?"

"What's that?" Liz replied.

"'Anything you say can and will be used against you in a court of law.'"

"Well, I have said a lot today, and I can't remember each comment."

"We will have to deal with each thing as we can remember them."

"Okay, and I need to prepare you for my dad."

"Prepare me in what way?"

"Well, his mind is gone, and you never know what's going to come out of his mouth."

"That won't be a problem in court because we will get a neurologist to testify that as you say his mind is gone."

As they walked up to Roscoe's room, they were stopped by a police officer.

"You will have to wait here,"

"I am his daughter, and this is his attorney," Liz said pointing at Josh with her thumb.

"Yeah, just hang on a second."

Detective Samms walked out of the Roscoe's room.

"I want to see my father," Liz said with her hands on her hips.

"Well, I see you lawyered up," Matt Samms said.

Josh Brahams looked at Liz and just slightly shook his head. She nodded her head slightly.

"I will answer any questions for Miss Gillette."

"I'm sure!" Matt Samms scoffed.

CHAPTER 30

2005

After the excitement over Eli's murder calmed down and about a month had passed, Detective Samms stopped making surprise visits when he figured out that Liz had followed the advice of her attorney and zipped her lips. He even tried some dirty tricks by threatening her with his goal being to scare the info out of her.

"Hi Liz," Matt said.

Liz sat with her lips sealed.

"You know, we are going to charge you with your mother's murder also."

Liz's eyes bulged out as far as they could go, but she said nothing. Then she realized that was a bluff. She raised her middle finger on her right hand and looked away from Matt.

"All right, Liz, you know you are making it worse on yourself by playing this game," he said.

Then he walked over to Liz and slapped across her face. She started to get worried. If he would do that, there might be no limit to the violence that he could impose on her. She picked up the phone and started dialing Josh Brahams number, but her glasses had been knocked off with the slap and she couldn't see the phone keys. Matt walked over to the old phone on the wall and with his index finger and thumb he unplugged the receiver plug that attached the handset to the wall phone. The phone was dead in her hand. That's when, Liz remembered the digital recorder that Josh Brahams had given her, and she switched it on because she knew that it was the one and only defense that she had. Then she took her hand out off her pocket and rested it on the table she was sitting in front of. Her hand just barely concealed the recorder.

"Look, Liz, I've been doing this a long time, and I know what I can get away with and what would sink my career. You don't have any signs of injury. That red face will fade before you could even dial 911. You can whine to your attorney as much as you want—No Proof! We will eventually prove that you or your father killed Mr. Animas. And you don't want your poor little daddy to go to prison! Do you? So why don't you just admit to this murder?" he said.

Liz was gritting her teeth so hard she could taste the mercury amalgam fillings. Then Liz stood up and backed out of the front door so that if he kept hitting her, there might be witnesses.

"Liz, come on. You and I both know that Eli used to kick your ass all the time so you were just getting vengeance when you picked up his gun. And then you made that convenient little scar on Roscoe's forehead to cover your tracks."

"No comment!" Liz muttered even though she didn't like saying that because guilty people often said that. Matt had followed her out of the house and that's when she heard it.

"Mom?"

Matt Samms cackled and said, "Oh, that is classic. Mom."

Now Liz was really worried, Roscoe had woken up from his nap and was looking for her. And Matt Samms was between the two of them.

"Leave us alone!" she said.

"You know how you could end all this trouble."

"Leave us alone!"

Just then another woman walked down the sidewalk. She was walking a chocolate Labrador. Matt glanced up at the interloper, and then looked at Liz to try and evaluate what she might do. When the woman heard, "Leave us alone," she could sense this was a bad situation and slowed her walk, constantly glancing from Matt to Liz. She saw that she was stuck in the middle of this confrontation. All three of them made eye contact, and Matt realized that this was going from bad to worse. He pulled his badge off his belt.

"This is a police matter, ma'am," he said, showing her his badge. Just as he said that, another voice threw a wrench into the scene.

"Mom?"

Liz's head snapped around and saw Roscoe on the porch of the house. Liz had to think quickly.

"Come on, Roscoe. Let's go play some music," she said.

As Matt was going through a long list of profanities in his head, Roscoe walked down off the porch and came to Liz's side. The woman was even more confused and wanted to get away from this crazy scene.

"Okay, everybody just relax. There's no problem here," Matt said.

Meanwhile, the woman had slid her hand into her purse and found a small can of mace, just in case. The woman looked at Matt and then said, "Sir, if you are a police officer, where is your uniform?"

"Just walk away from this ma'am," Matt said.

She looked at Liz, and for just a second, she thought that Liz's face looked red on one side.

"Are you okay?" the woman asked Liz.

"No," Liz said.

That really brought the woman's caution senses to high alert. Her dog sensed trouble that only a dog could detect. The dog immediately started barking at Matt. He was not happy because his plan was falling apart. Matt decided he had to take decisive action, he reached for the gun in his shoulder holster. The woman saw this coming and quickly unloaded the pepper spray container in Matt's eyes. At the same time, the dog clamped down on his ankle.

"Run!" the woman shouted.

"No, my car," Liz said.

"Cooper! Come on," the woman screamed.

Matt was feeling around on the ground for his gun which he had dropped. He still couldn't see.

The woman forced her dog into the back seat of the car and then she climbed in beside him. Liz talked Roscoe into the front passenger seat, but that took longer than it should have. Liz threw the car into gear and floored it. Matt now had the gun in his hands when he heard the squealing tires, he pointed it at the noise but knew better than firing a round blind.

The sound of the tires and the cursing from Matt Samms caused several people in the neighborhood of Rosebud street to call the police. Matt Samms had struggled to his feet and he was able to get back to his car and drove away as the responding officers pulled up in front of 136 Rosebud. responding to the property had become routine for one of the officers, who responded to the death of Eli. No one knew where the problem was so they went to the house across the street from Liz's house. The other two officers went to houses where the calls had come from.

Matt Samms drove a few blocks away and turned right around the corner. Once there, he stopped and got a bottle of water and rinsed his eyes as thoroughly as possible. He was angry at himself for not having his sunglasses on which would have defeated the majority of the pepper spray. But he knew where Liz lived, and this was far from over and he knew how to seek vengeance on Liz. He committed himself to throwing one or both of them into prison. Yes, that would absolve him from any connection to this case.

After driving away from the scene of the attack, Liz dropped the woman and her dog off a few houses from their residence and then drove to a hotel across town. She checked in with Roscoe under an assumed name.

"Okay, Miss Barbarso, that will be one hundred and thirty dollars, and your room number will be 320."

"Thank you, sir. Come on, Roscoe!"

Roscoe got up off the bench and joined Liz who assumed the name of Becky like her mom. She had changed Roscoe's name, too, because she assumed that Matt Samms would be looking for her. But Roscoe wasn't up to the trickery.

"Mom, what did you call me?"

Liz just put her had on his shoulder. "It's okay, Dad. We need to go up to our room."

When Liz got up to the room, she got on the phone and set up two important meetings. The first with a recording studio and the second was with a realtor. Liz wanted to do some recordings. Roscoe had been writing some songs too. And even though Liz didn't know these songs, she worked hard to learn them and the rest she had written on paper. They started with one session recording songs from the sixties, seventies, and eighties. It took all day, but they put down a lot of cover songs.

Matt Samms called all the hotels in town. He asked if they had Liz and Roscoe Gillette staying there.

"I'm sorry, sir. We can't give out the names of our guests."

"Well I'm a detective with the police department, and we are looking for a murderer."

"Detective, you need to come in and show us some ID before we can help you."

"We are looking for a young girl with a mentally challenged older man."

"No, I haven't seen anyone like that."

But the last place he called, when he made that last statement, the desk clerk chuckled, and Matt knew he had got them. He drove over to that hotel in question and parked outside to watch the place. Matt felt justified in doing this because he knew that one of these two were the murderer. But as the day got late, he thought he had been duped. He left ten minutes before Liz and Roscoe returned from their very long day of recording. They were tired and went straight to their room. The next day would be a recording of Roscoe's original songs.

To pay for this, Liz went to the bank and took out a loan against the sale of the house and then she talked to the realtor and got the sale started. Liz paid the recording studio, but they were definitely taking a lot of chances. Everything had to come together for this to work.

At the recording studio, they met a manager of bands, and he liked their work, but they had to put down more money to make thousands of copies of their songs which the manager sent all over the world to contacts at radio stations. And even though the act was not picking up in the States, in South Africa and Australia, it was wildly popular, and they stared cranking out thousands of CDs. The songs were playing on the radio and selling out almost as soon as they came in.

Liz had to quickly come up with a name for the group because you couldn't have a band without a name. Roscoe came up with the name when he said, "The sky is falling." Liz suddenly realized that it could be a workable name, but it just didn't feel right. Although it did describe the last year in their lives perfectly. The two were sitting in their hotel room when Roscoe said, "Pieces of sky," and suddenly, both of the singers knew that they have a name for their band. Pieces of Sky was born. Liz still couldn't believe the moments of brilliance that came out of his brain. And then he would drop back into his dementia state.

CHAPTER 31

2005

Money was beginning to come in, and the manager of the band was very happy, the distributor was pleased, and Liz found and selected other members of the group. The group Pieces of Sky were becoming known all over the world. The group now consisted of five members. With Liz and Roscoe on lead, Roscoe on piano, a drummer, a bass player, lead guitarist, and the band was complete. The manager was working full time to take the act international, and he had already made commitments in South Africa for large concerts and smaller venues. The gears were turning, and all the important decisions were being made. Liz and Roscoe and some of the other band members met with the manager on a weekly basis. They rehearsed twice a week and played smaller venues at least once a week, just to keep their act sharp. There had been no sign of Matt Samms since the incident at Liz's house, but Liz kept looking over her shoulder every time they were out, expecting him to show up when they least expected it.

They managed to sell the house, which was a sad day for Liz, but she knew this day was coming, especially since they lived in hotels most of the time now. The manager was responsible for setting all that up; he had hotels scheduled out for weeks in advance. They travelled in a bus when they were in the States, and then they flew when they went international. This was the life of music acts worldwide, and Roscoe seemed to thrive on this lifestyle. Liz wondered if he had any memories of the early days of the Backdoor Brothers.

THE GATE WAS OPEN

Liz made it a habit to share a room with Roscoe because she was worried about him and didn't think he could handle living by himself. One day, they were sitting in their hotel room, and Liz asked Roscoe a question.

"I have wanted to ask you this question for a long time now, but decided to wait till a time when there were less cops around every corner."

"Umm, humm," Roscoe made an affirmative noise.

"What happened between you and Eli?" Liz inquired.

Roscoe appeared to be confused and lacking understanding. "What?" he said.

"You know, that day when all the police came to the house, and they took you to the police station and asked you all of those questions."

Roscoe just shook his head back and forth and stared at Liz. "I don't know," he said.

"The day Eli died. You remember Eli, don't you?"

Then Roscoe started nodding, and he put his hands together with his palms touching and looked at the ceiling. Liz's eyes were bulging out of her eye sockets as she watched a most amazing transformation. His fingers were pointing up and they created a steeple with his fingers.

"The gate was open," Roscoe said.

Liz's mouth dropped open as Roscoe looked up toward the ceiling.

"Did you shoot him?" Liz asked.

Roscoe sat there with his hands together and stared straight at Liz.

"Did you pull the trigger?"

"Mom?"

Liz was still shocked by this revelation. She shook her head to compose herself.

Then she closed her eyes and rubbed the palm of her left hand across her left cheek and around to the back of her neck. Liz spent hours rolling this around in her brain. It seemed that Roscoe thought that he had sent Eli to heaven, but they had never discussed religion.

Then she realized something else. Roscoe's use of the word *mom* was a way he used of disarming people.

That's when Liz stared directly back into Roscoe's eyes, and for the first time, she suddenly saw a deep understanding in those eyes. Roscoe wasn't in another universe; he was right here on earth. She shook her head and just stared at him. She didn't know how to broach this topic, and she didn't want to question his veracity. But she was sensing some dishonesty—or was it just a lack of cognitive understanding? This put Liz in a huge dilemma.

"You understand me, don't you?" she said.

Roscoe just smiled at her, still looking casually at his daughter.

"Has this whole thing been a huge scam?" Liz said.

"Mom?" Roscoe said.

Liz pointed at Roscoe. "And enough of that Mom shit."

Roscoe looked down at the ground.

"Roscoe, you are driving me crazy!" she screamed.

"No, Liz. This is not a scam. I was trying to protect us, and now that we are leaving the States, I am more comfortable leveling with you," Roscoe said.

Liz just starred wide-eyed at the man who was sitting in front of her.

"You are speaking normally, intelligently." Tears started to fall out of Liz's eyes.

"I am so sorry it upset you, sweetie," Roscoe said.

"I can't believe you could keep this travesty going this long."

"And the hardest part was what this would do to you."

"So you don't have dementia?"

"Oh, I do!"

"How can you say that? It is a lie!"

"No, honey. It's not. Eventually, it will happen."

"Well, yeah, eventually, we will all have this disease. I knew you couldn't have remembered all those songs."

"No. You see, Liz, I drop into and out of dementia."

"And where are you now?"

"Since I am having this conversation with you, I would say I am out of it."

"Oh my god, you are saying that you could forget everything I am saying in a fraction of a second?"

"No, I am not saying that. It usually takes longer than that."

"How long does it take?"

"Years."

"So for two or three years, you are normal," she said, using air quotes, "and then for two or three years, you are gone?"

"Liz, this just started, so I don't know how it will progress, but it seems music is the one thing that doesn't leave me, and maybe music is the one thing that can bring me out of this nightmare."

"I can't believe that I am having this conversation with you! This is insane!" she shouted.

"Yes, I know that it is very confusing, and I am confused also."

"So now you have your mind back how far back can you remember?"

"I can remember everything that anybody can remember."

"So do you remember when I was conceived?"

"Well, I was very young then, and I wasn't very wise to the ways of the world."

"Boy, I'll say," Liz rebuked.

"I really didn't understand birth control. I was only sixteen, but I have tried to take on more responsibility and do right by you."

"You know, it would have been cool, if you would have done right by my mom and helped with medical care. You have been rolling in dough, and you could have easily helped. And by the way, now that your mind is back, do you remember where all your cash is stashed?"

"Mostly," he said.

"And how long have you been back to reality?"

"For the last few weeks, but I couldn't reveal this with that detective putting the screws down on us."

"Yeah, that is for sure, but what are we going to do in the future? Are we going to stay out of the States?"

"Well, we will have to discuss that and let's see how South Africa treats us."

"So now that you, quote-unquote, have your mind back…did you kill Eli?"

Roscoe glanced around to see if anyone was in earshot. Then he walked over to Liz and whispered in her ear. Liz had been shocked by the violence of that day, but this latest revelation was equally shocking.

There is no way Roscoe could have taken on Eli, she thought.

"Who are you?" Liz replied.

"Now who has dementia? You can't even remember my name?"

"Oh, I remember the name that you gave me and the story that you told me, but now I am wondering if any of it is true."

The man laughed and looked into her eyes. "Well, if that detective shows up before we catch our flight, you won't be asking these questions."

"Wait a minute, what does law enforcement have to do with you deceiving me?"

"No one is deceiving you. At least, not me."

"How do I know you are really my father?"

"We did a DNA test, didn't we?"

Liz walked out of the hotel room in a major quandary. She made a beeline for the hospital and had six hours before the flight left, so she hoped the she could make this connection. She went to John Morris's office and asked the receptionist if she could see John. The receptionist said she would have to wait for two hours, but at that point, they had a cancellation and they could get her in then. Liz went down to the cafeteria and waited until the two hours passed. Then she came back and John could see her.

"Hi, Liz. What's up?"

"I need your help, John," she replied.

"Okay."

"So guess what!"

"What?"

"Roscoe doesn't have Alzheimer's."

"Ah…what?"

"He can now speak in a clear and intelligent way," she said.

"Explain."

"He told me he goes in and out of dementia. Is that possible?"

"Well, no. Alzheimer's is like coral. If a human hand touches coral, it is gone forever. It will never come back."

"Can you think of any way he could have temporary dementia?"

"Well…there are always people that change the rules for every disorder. People survive cancer, and there was a disease in Europe that took out seventy-five percent of the population. But somehow, twenty-five percent were unaffected by the Black Death and survived. So I wouldn't be surprised by anything. Also there are certain medications that can cause temporary dementia in some people. But we tested Roscoe for those medications and didn't find any of those, so I guess this is a medical mystery," John said.

"He says playing music helps him with his dementia."

"Wow. I have never heard that, but maybe he is the first case of music-relieved dementia. Someone has to be first. Also, Liz, stress can cause temporary dementia in some people.

"So basically, what you are saying is maybe it is possible."

"No. What I am saying is maybe anything is possible, I have just never heard of it. One thing that is out there is some Alzheimer's patients regain some cognitive abilities, but the bad part of this story is that most people who regain some of their memory often die shortly after."

"What? So you are saying that Roscoe is on death's door?"

"No, I am just telling you what research has shown. Roscoe's case could be totally different. I don't think the science has caught up with this, but just be aware of all the possibilities. You don't want to be taken by surprise."

"Well, the surprise has come and gone. I just picked my jaw up off the floor. Well, maybe it was the stress of dealing with Eli, because now he can remember and perform hundreds of songs."

"You know after this tour is over you should look into getting him into a study because he is definitely a unique individual. When does the tour start?"

"A couple of hours."

"And you are okay with that?'

"This is like a runaway train. I really don't have any control over it. We are committed to it, but I am worried that I don't know this man. Who is this man, John?"

"Well, he is your father. There is no way to alter DNA results."

"I know that."

"You know, lots of musical acts continue to perform but don't get along very well. It's all about the money."

"Okay, well, I guess I will just have to bite the bullet and get through this tour. But what do I do if he drops back into dementia?"

"Well, Liz, you have been playing with Roscoe for a long time, and you are an expert at dealing with his dementia. The only thing that you have to get good at is figuring out is which Roscoe you are dealing with," John said.

"Okay, John. Well, talking with you always calms me down. Thank you."

"You are welcome, Liz. Have a great tour!"

CHAPTER 32

1957

At a very young age Roscoe developed a super memory. He could outdo most of his teachers and was put into the gifted program. The ten year old walked into the classroom with his arms straight down at his side. His walk was very robotic and his lips, were moving slightly as he worked his way through a mathematical equation in his mind. When he got to his locker he stood at the metal door and sketched out the numbers on his locker. There ere some disparaging comments written on the door by the bully's in the school. It was class change time and all the students were streaming through the halls. Roscoe Gillette stood there talking to himself and occasionally pushed his glasses up as they slid down his nose. A couple of thugs were walking down the hallway when Roscoe was standing in front of his locker.

"Hey look at this geek," Tommy said.

The football linebacker with biceps the size of canalopes pushed Roscoe into his locker as he and his girlfriend laughed. Tommy's friends were backing him up and they all joined in on the laughter. His girlfriend had a vice grip on his hand, which was her attempt to solidify and ensure the relationship. His crew giggled with his pseudo toughness. Tommy broke free of his girlfriends grip and then walked up behind Roscoe and with one size thirteen shoe he placed a slight tap into the bends of Roscoe's knee. This caused the ten year olds knees to buckle and he toppled back like a 2x4 and when his back hit the floor his head snapped back and hit the hard tile floor too.

Tommy would often force Roscoe to do his homework for him and even do a couple take home tests for him. But now Roscoe lay bleeding on the floor as the rest of the students scattered. The science teacher walked up to the supine boy and saw the blood.

"Somebody get the school nurse."

The teacher tried to arouse him by shaking his shoulders, but got no response.

Roscoe woke up in the hospital.

"Hey how ya doing buddy?" his father said when his eye's opened.

"Who are you?" Roscoe inquired.

"Ha ha, he is a real joker. How are you feeling son?"

"A little dizzy."

"Well we are going to get you out of this hospital, because a little exercise will do you a world of good."

For the next year Roscoe remained a little foggy. The concussion left it's mark on him both physically and mentally. For the rest of his time in school, he was just an average student. The straight A's were left in a puddle of blood on the floor that the janitor cleaned up.

The next year Roscoe started to play in the school band, he tried the accordion and then found the piano. Nobody in the school ever identified Tommy as the person who caused the injury to Roscoe. But that concussion definitely ended his days of high intelligence and forced him to struggle in school. But his solace was the music that he thrived at. He would be playing every free minute that he had and it was the one thing that he still enjoyed at school.

A lot of his teachers wondered what his teachers wondered what had happened to the formerly brilliant, attentive student that scored so high on every test. And now was an average student, playing music really helped him and he became quite the musician. Roscoe now seemed distracted and aloof. His grades were now average at best and music was his savior as he entered a new chapter in his life. The bully's left him alone now because he couldn't help them with their schoolwork anymore and the teachers were watching the students to see if they could solve this crime. But no one ever came forward with information and the event was eventually forgotten.

THE GATE WAS OPEN

The concussion had ruined some aspects of Roscoe's super memory but it also helped him in other ways, Now he couldn't do math or think scientifically but his memory for song lyres was incredible. Roscoe was suffering in a lot of his subjects and his super memory which he had used to amaze a lot of his friends by remembering each students birthday and what happened on a certain day two years ago. He lost most of this abilities but his hippocampus was stronger then ever and he could retain song lyrics from every song he had ever heard. The young man often escaped to his piano to get away from his mother's alcoholism. The only problem was it was in his aunts basement. Roscoe would go over to his aunts house and ring the doorbell. If his aunt was home she would let him go downstairs and practice. It was his way to avoid turmoil in his life. When his aunt wasn't home home he figured out a way to squeeze his body through one of the small basement windows in his aunt's house. Then when he started middle school the music teacher had a piano in the classroom that he used for classes. Roscoe took every music class that he could and the teacher took an affinity to him, he was the protege of everything musical. The music teacher actually learned some things from Roscoe, who was like a young Wolfgang Amadeus Mozart. As the boy got deeper and deeper into music theory, he started writing songs but during those early years there wasn't much interest in his songs. The music teacher was amazed at the boys innate abilities. When Roscoe turned fifteen he started the Backdoor Brothers and the rest is history.

"So when can you come in?" John inquired.

"Right now?" Roscoe said.

"Well I can't do it today." John laughed.

"Ok you pick the time." The older man stated.

"How about tomorrow?"

"What time?"

"One o'clock work for you?"

"Sure, I'll see you then."

John hung up the phone and picked up a pad a started furiously jotting down some notes. This could be the opportunity of his career. To have a formerly confirmed case of Alzheimer's which back to clear cognitive thought was unheard of. Even thoug he had been studying geriatric medicine medicine for many years and still he was stunned that this could happen. He saw a possible PhD in his future if he could write his thesis on this incredible event.

Roscoe showed up at John's office in the hospital. He was wearing dark shades and a hat.

"Why the disguise?" John asked.

"Law enforcement is still looking for me."

"Yes and meeting with you is putting me in a bad position."

"Well we can make this fast if you just take me to financial services."

"Can I just ask you a few questions first?"

"Of course, you have been very helpful to my daughter, so it's the leastI can do."

"First, I am going to give you a small test, okay?"

"I guess." Roscoe said.

"I want you to remember these four words, Apple, Clarity, Mr. Robinson, and Tunnel."

"You know you need to mix up your memory tests."

"So you remember from the last time I tested you?"

"I have a recollection."

"So what is your daughters name?"

"Come on John, you can't be serious I remembered that when I was in the depths of dementia."

"So you refer to it as dementia and not Alzheimer's dementia?"

"John, what I am going through is clearly a different kind of demetia."

"So I've heard you claimed that it comes and goes, that's incredibly unique."

"Yea that is exactly what happens,"

"Well. it's not going to be called Alzheimer's any more, maybe Gillete's."

"Can you help me understand exactly how your dementia can be so intermittent."

"John you are the scientist I am just a musician."

"I have heard that you are a lot more than just a musician." John retorted.

"Well I don't know about that."

"I knew you when you were fully involved in everything that goes along with dementia."

"Is that right?" Roscoe replied.

"So now I am wondering if you were just playing me and the entire system before. I mean that would have kept you out of a long prison sentence."

"That's a great question, John."

"So how is Liz doing?"

Roscoe just stared at him in silence with the shift in topic. He felt that John was trying to keep him talking here and maybe Matt Samms was going to walk through that door next.

"Liz is fine, she is playing and singing and she has a very loyal following in South Africa."

"Can you tell me what happened with that guy she was dating here?"

"Who was that?"

"Are you saying you don't remember Eli Animas?"

Roscoe just shrugged his shoulders.

"Doesn't ring a bell."

"Well someone killed him in Liz's house, do you remember that?"

"Can't say that I do."

John looked at Roscoe and detected a slight smile across his lips. John's mind was spinning like a top. What was real and what was fake.

Is this intermittent dementia flaring up again? Is this a real thing or is this all an elaborate hoax by a mastermind of deception?' John thought. Who really pulled the trigger in the death of Eli animas?

"Well I will give you directions to the financial department." John said.

"Can't you just take me there?"

"Sorry but I have a meeting that I have to attend." John said.

"Okay well where am I going?"

"Third floor, walk down the hallway to 3304."
"Well thank you John."
"Good luck Roscoe in all your endeavors."

The elderly man walked out the door and headed for the elevator. When he got to the room with the number 3304 on it, he was a little confused. It did not say financial department on it. But he opened the door and it was dark in the room. In an instant an arm shot out of the darkness and grabbed his wrist.

"What's happening?" Roscoe said.
"Don't pull that dementia bullshit on me again." Detective Samms said as he slid the cuffs on.
"I'm afraid you have the wrong person." Roscoe stuttered.
"No I've been waiting a long time for this Mr. Gillette.
"To whom do I owe the pleasure?"
"Detective Matt Samms, Carolina Beach police department."
"I don't know what's going on here."
"Oh I think you do."
"My daughter will be very upset with this."
"Is that right, well maybe we should ask her ..."
"Don't worry daddy it will be okay."
That was followed by the sound of tears and sobbing.
"Liz?"

EPILOGUE

Carolina Beach was on the Atlantic Ocean and there was a harbor where all the fishing boats were moored. Every morning the boats headed out at six A.M. The Box Elder was a fishing boat and each boat tried to find a different location and hopefully they would hit the motherlode and pull in a huge catch. They waited to see where the other boats were headed and then choose their own direction.

At two miles out they passed a large island of floating plastic bottles, bags, and other trash. This island was the size of a small city and they were on the edge of it and stayed there because cutting through the middle of this plastic pile of filth would cause the engines to foul. It took thirty minutes to pass into to open water. The habit of this planet to befoul the oceans with the waste of seven billion humans in one giant cesspool. Out of sight out of mind is killing this planet. At three miles out the Box Elder was alone and they cut the engines and were drifting.

Cole Ash was the captain and he climbed the flying bridge and scanning the surrounding ocean when Cole saw the shark fin.

"Head north, I can see a shark and you guys know how much a shark fin will sell for." Cole said.

"Is this the place where you saw the shark?" the first mate asked.

"Yeah." Cole responded as he cut the engines.

About a half a mile out was a cruise ship and many passengers were standing on the deck gazing out at the fishing boat. Three of the crew were staring at the surface of the ocean when the first mate grabbed Cole's arm and said.

"What is that?"

The body was floating in a position that looked like he was on a crucifix. The body was face down and had about a dozen hard shelled crabs hanging on to it and feeding off the body and the other algae that was clinging to the body. Cole walked up to the rail with a twelve gauge shotgun. He pumped it and aimed.

If I kill the shark we will be able to recover the body and get the fin off the shark, the captain thought.

Three loud booms sounded across the water and the shark floated lifeless to the surface. The crew hefted the shark and the dead body on board. The man was completely pale. There was a gunshot wound in the white shirt in the of his chest. His identification tag was attached to the pocket of his suit coat.

"Detective" ... then he wiped the scum off the name tag with his thumb. "Matt Samms, Carolina Beach Police Department."

"Well In guess he was sleeping with the fishes," the first mate said.

"We are three miles out so we are out of any jurisdiction of the police."

"So who then, the coast guard?"

"Yup," Cole said.

When the 737 touched down in Johannesburg, South Africa, Roscoe and Liz walked off the plane. They sat down at a table and started talking. "What are we going to do now?" Liz asked.

"Well this country will extradite us back to the U.S."

"Yeah and now both of us have blood on our hands."

"So we are going to catch a bus to Botswanna because they have no extradition agreement with the U.S.

Liz and Roscoe crossed the border into Botswanna. With in a year they opened a company that took people on safaris. They also sang in a bar of the local hotel.

The End

ABOUT THE AUTHOR

Ken England has spent many years exploring this world, from eight years as an instructor and course director with the Voyageur Outward Bound School to travels around this earth. He's visited deserts, mountains, jungles, and the tundra of the Northwest Territories, and he has followed adventure in all these environments. He's paddled rivers from Mexico to the Arctic. After his time as an adventurer, he became a paramedic in many places around the United States before he settled in Bozeman, Montana, and started the paramedic service there. He now volunteers for the American Red Cross and travels to disasters all across the country.

CPSIA information can be obtained
at www.ICGtesting.com
Printed in the USA
JSHW020727050523
41292JS00001B/40